SWITCH ON TO LOVE

Madge Fairley enjoys her work as secretary to television producer Miles Brent, although she is sad that he has fallen under the spell of the selfish actress Patricia Carnford. When Jim Lingard gives up his job in the family business to try his luck at acting, Madge is distressed, as Jim's previous experience has only been on the amateur stage. However, for Madge's sake, Miles Brent gives Jim a part in a television play, but this leads to disillusionment and much heart-searching for Madge.

M.R.J.

IRENE LAWRENCE

◆

SWITCH ON TO LOVE

Complete and Unabridged

LINFORD
Leicester

First published in Great Britain

First Linford Edition
published December 1993

Copyright © 1967 by Irene Lawrence

British Library CIP Data

Lawrence, Irene
Switch on to love.—Large print ed.—
Linford romance library
I. Title II. Series
823.914 [F]

ISBN 0–7089–7470–8

Published by
F. A. Thorpe (Publishing) Ltd.
Anstey, Leicestershire

Set by Words & Graphics Ltd.
Anstey, Leicestershire
Printed and bound in Great Britain by
T. J. Press (Padstow) Ltd., Padstow, Cornwall

This book is printed on acid-free paper

1

IT was dark in the producer's box overlooking the studio.

Through the big plate-glass window, Madge Fairley, staring down, could see the confusion of furniture, scenery, half-built sets and cameras, which, when she had first come to Metropolitan Television, had so amazed her. It had seemed absolutely impossible, she had thought, that order could ever come out of such chaos.

But now she was used to it. Now she thought it nothing out of the ordinary to see a play being rehearsed in one corner of the enormous studio, a comedy act in another and perhaps a juggler performing in another.

And all the time men and women, apparently in a frantic hurry, scurried here and there, while camera crews took up their positions and sound technicians and continuity and make-up girls went from set to set, checking, advising, scolding.

"What in blazes does Charles think he's doing?" Miles Brent growled.

He was sitting beside Madge, watching the two lovers on the screen before him.

"You're the only woman I've ever loved," came the man's voice as he gazed down at the pretty girl in his arms.

"He might as well be clasping a dish-mop, for all the passion he has in his voice," the producer snapped and, switching on the microphone at his side, he said sharply: "Charles, old man, let's have some feeling, please. You're supposed to be declaring your undying love for Peggy, not asking her to wash out a couple of shirts. Start again, and for pity's sake put some life into it!"

The couple repeated the scene and, at last, Miles said, "That'll do for today, thanks. We'll have another run through in the morning."

Glancing at Madge he grinned, a grin which lit up his tense, rather solemn face under the crisp, dark hair. "I could do with a cup of tea, Madge! What about it?" He had a deep, pleasant voice.

"I'll bring it into your office in five minutes," she promised, and stood up.

Hurrying along the narrow corridor, with its plain white walls and closed doors, Madge marvelled once again at the circumstances which had brought her to such interesting surroundings.

Six months ago she had been a shorthand typist, working for the sales manager of a northern factory. She had been quite happy, living at home with her widowed mother and seeing her boyfriend, Jim Lingard — who worked in his father's printing firm — two or three times a week.

Although Jim had not made an official proposal, it was generally accepted he would do so in due course. It seemed as if her life had been worked out for her. She would save hard, so that she and Jim would eventually be able to afford a little house on the outskirts of Hunsworth. Later on, they would have children — two or perhaps even three. If the future was unexciting, it was nevertheless not displeasing to Madge.

Then Jenny's letter had come — Jenny Briggs who had left Hunsworth a year before.

Madge and Jenny had grown up together in the same street and had gone to the same school. But Jenny was the restless type, yearning after the excitement to be found in a big city. After an unhappy romance she had found herself a job in London and had written to Madge, describing excitedly the new world she had entered as secretary to a dress designer.

I've taken a flat and it has an extra room, Madge, she had written. *So if you think of getting a job in London*

*you won't even have to find any digs,
just move into my spare room!*

Madge had smiled over the letter and
had thought nothing more of it until,
quite suddenly, her mother died.

When the first stage of her grief was
past, Madge had to ask herself what
she intended to do now. She could no
longer afford to pay the rent of the
house in which she and her mother
had lived for so long. Surely, now
that she was alone, Jim would want to
marry her and take care of her. But he
was curiously evasive when she hinted
that it was time they settled down.
He was seeing less of her these days,
too, because he had joined an amateur
dramatic society and rehearsals for the
current production took up most of his
spare time.

Rather hurt, Madge had written
on impulse applying for a job with
Metropolitan Television, having seen
an advertisement in the morning newspaper for shorthand typists. She had

been asked to go for an interview and, to her astonishment, had been offered a job immediately in the typing pool.

She had not returned to Hunsworth but had asked a friend of her mother's to send her things on. She had dropped a line to Jim who, rather to her dismay, had shown no disappointment at her decision, but had actually congratulated her on what she had done. Rather mysteriously, he said he hoped to see her sooner than she expected.

Jenny, of course, had welcomed Madge rapturously and her friend wondered if, in spite of her wonderful job, Jenny was perhaps not just a little bit lonely.

The job with The Metropolitan Television Company was interesting, as Madge soon found. Her work in the typing pool took her into the offices of the producers and other executives. One week she worked exclusively for Miles Brent, because his secretary had 'flu.

Miles had found her quick and intelligent and, when his secretary had left to get married, he had asked Madge to step into her job.

Collecting two cups of tea and a plate of biscuits from the tea trolley at the end of the corridor, Madge made for the room she shared with Miles Brent.

A girl was seated in the leather armchair by the producer's desk. She turned round as Madge entered.

"Oh, it's you!" she said, looking disappointed. "Where's Mr. Brent?"

"He'll be along in a few minutes, Miss Carnford," Madge replied. "Will you have a cup of tea?"

"Thanks!"

Handing her own cup over, Madge placed the other on Miles Brent's desk.

As she went to her own desk at the other side of the room she found herself wondering why she felt an instinctive dislike for this girl, who was engaged to the young producer.

Patricia Carnford was well known to television viewers as the girlfriend of Ray Felton, the tough 'private eye'.

Week after week she found herself in the most impossible situations; but she always remained cool and calm, not a curl of her very fair hair out of place at the end of each adventure.

A couple of minutes later Miles Brent came bustling into the office. Madge saw the quick frown as he looked across the room and saw Patricia sitting beside his desk. But this quickly disappeared as he went forward.

"Pat, darling! I didn't know you were looking in."

"You sound almost disappointed," she said.

He kissed her uplifted cheek. "I'm always glad to see you Pat, though if you think I've finished for the day, I'm afraid I've another couple of hours' work to do."

She pouted up at him. "But Jimmy Grayson's giving a cocktail party at the Lansbury Hotel. I want to go!"

"I'm sorry, but it's impossible!" Seeing the angry glitter in her eyes, he added: "You go ahead by taxi and

I'll try to get there before it finishes."

She seemed about to say something else, but then glanced at Madge and stood up, drawing her fur coat about her.

"I dare say Roger's going," she said coldly. "I'll go along to his office and see. I don't expect he'll advise me to take a taxi to the other side of London." She swept out of the room.

Roger Peterson — who starred with Patricia Carnford in *Ray Felton, Private Eye* — was very good-looking and rumour had it that he was as much in love with Patricia in reality as he pretended to be on the screen.

"You'd better take these letters, Madge," Miles said, and Madge thought he looked rather sad.

As she reached for her notebook, she glanced at her watch. Half-past five already! Oh, well, it was one of the things Miles had warned her about when he had offered to take her on as his secretary. "Lots of work, my bad temper and a certainty that you'll never know when you're going to finish a long day's work," he had said.

Madge checked a sigh. She and Jenny had hoped to go to the cinema that evening. Oh, well, they could go another night.

But, as Miles began to dictate, she decided she had better give Jenny a ring later and suggest she went to the cinema on her own.

★ ★ ★

It was seven o'clock before Miles finished dictating, and Madge was feeling very tired. She still had the long journey across London ahead of her, and the prospect was most uninviting. However, at least she was to be spared the ordeal of queuing for a bus.

"Now, the least I can do is to drive you home," Miles said unexpectedly.

"I can easily get a bus," Madge protested, "and you have to go to that cocktail party."

"I'll go on there afterwards," Miles

said, escorting her to the car park and seating her in his rather old-fashioned limousine.

They chatted easily throughout the journey and Madge found herself liking Miles more and more. Though he was an important executive with MTV, and engaged to Patricia Carnford, so lovely and successful, she suspected that at heart he was a lonely, rather introverted man.

On impulse, when they drew up outside the house where she and Jenny had their second-floor flat, she asked him if he had time to go in with her for a drink.

"I think we have some sherry," she said with a twinkle that warmed her soft brown eyes and brought to life dimples in each rounded cheek.

He frowned. "I really ought to get on to the cocktail party, but . . . " Suddenly he was jumping out of the car and hurrying round to open the door on Madge's side. "I'd love to come in with you for a few minutes,"

11

he said. "If Pat's with Roger Peterson she's probably forgotten all about me by this time. In any case, I've never met your friend, Jenny. She sounds quite a character from what you've told me."

As they entered the house and climbed the two flights of stairs. Madge was glad she had rung up earlier. Jenny had told her then that she preferred not to go to the cinema alone and would have something ready to eat when Madge got home.

The flat occupied the whole of the second floor. There was a big sitting-room at the front, overlooking the street, with a tiny kitchen adjacent. The two bedrooms and bathroom were at the back.

Jenny was in the kitchen when Madge showed Miles into the sitting-room.

"There's a letter for you on the mantelpiece!" she called and Madge, glancing towards the fireplace, recognized Jim's handwriting on the envelope propped against the clock.

"We have a visitor!" she called back,

and Jenny appeared in the kitchen doorway.

Her mouth fell open, seeing Miles standing beside her friend. "Good heavens, a handsome man!" she gasped. "Where did you find him, Madge?"

Madge laughed. "This is Mr. Brent, my boss. And don't stand there looking like a stranded goldfish, Jenny!"

Jenny came forward with an out-stretched hand. She was a tall girl with a mop of red hair and a pair of perpetually twinkling green eyes. Her skin was freckled, her mouth a little too big. She was plain and knew it. She was also one of the kindest, happiest people Madge had ever met.

"I hope you like fish pie, Mr. Brent," she said, shaking hands with him.

"I'm not stopping more than a few minutes," Miles said — but, as he looked round the big homely room, there was a wistful look in his eyes.

Madge produced the sherry and three glasses and they solemnly toasted one another.

"What kind of work do you do, Miss Briggs?" Miles asked, stretching comfortably in the rather sagging arm-chair.

"The name's Jenny," she said. "As for the job, I'm secretary to Madame Dumier, the dress designer."

"It must be an interesting job," Miles murmured.

"It has its points. At any rate, I'm usually back here by six o'clock." The severity with which she said this was softened by the twinkle in her green eyes.

Miles grinned. "Yes, I know I keep Madge longer than I should," he said. "But I warned her before she took the job on."

"You've no right to say that, Jenny!" Madge cried. "I love my job. I wouldn't change it for the world — or a ten to five job like yours!"

"Calm down and have some more sherry!" Jenny offered, unperturbed. "Indignation and drink have put quite a colour into your cheeks."

Madge, meeting Miles's eyes, flushed even more. Did he suspect that she had been complaining to her friend about the long hours she had to work? If so, she longed to tell him that it wasn't true.

But Miles was not thinking anything of the kind. He was wondering why he had never realized before how pretty Madge was, with her glossy fair hair and soft hazel eyes.

Suddenly he stood up. "I must go," he said. "At this rate, I'll not be in time to collect my fiancée when the cocktail party ends."

"So you're engaged!" Jenny wailed. "How is it I never get to meet any unattached men these days? I think I'll go back to Yorkshire."

Miles grinned and sniffed appreciatively, with a glance at the kitchen door.

"If you can cook as well as I believe you can," he laughed, "I don't think you'll be single for very long."

Both girls went downstairs to see him off. When he had driven away Jenny

15

slipped her arm through Madge's, and they went back to the flat.

"I like your boss," she said. "He seems pretty easy to get along with."

"I hope he didn't take your remarks about my working late too seriously," Madge said.

"Of course he didn't! He can see for himself that you're the type to work your fingers to the bone for any man you've taken a fancy to."

Madge couldn't help but laugh. "Oh, Jenny, you are the limit!" she cried. "I wonder if I'll ever be able to take you seriously."

"You'd better read your letter while I dish up," Jenny said as they entered the flat again.

Why should Jim be writing again so soon after his last letter? Madge wondered, as she opened the envelope.

She had heard from him only a few days ago. He rarely wrote more than once a fortnight.

She read the few scrawled lines.

Darling Madge, Jim wrote. *You will be surprised to hear that I have at last made up my mind to throw in my job at the printing works and try to make a go of it on the stage. As you know, I've been in several local productions in the last year and both the reporter on the local newspaper and others, who should know say I have quite a future on the stage, if I'm prepared to work.*

So I've told Dad I'm going to London for a bit, to see if I can get a part or two and widen my experience. Of course, he's upset, for he thought I'd take the business on when he retired. But my mind's made up. It won't be long before you see me.

Love,

Jim

Madge read the letter through again, then stared, aghast, ahead of her. What did this mean? Surely Jim couldn't be so foolish as to think he could throw up a secure future and make a name in the most uncertain profession of all — the theatre.

Once or twice she had seen him in shows given by the Hunsworth Thespian Society. She had thought he was good for an amateur, but there had been others appearing with him who had been quite as good, if not better.

Since coming to London to work in television she had seen dozens of men and women, who appeared day after day at the studios to appear in small parts, or just to sit about and hope something would be found for them.

Surely Jim wasn't going to join that hopeless band?

Why, he had everything to hope for in Hunsworth — his father's business to run as he liked when Mr. Lingard retired, his amateur dramatics to interest him in his spare time, a host of friends . . .

"Well, what's he been saying this time?" Jenny asked, coming into the room carrying a large dish. "Surely he hasn't asked you to marry him at long last!"

"Jim is absolutely crazy," Madge cried, her eyes flashing with anger. "He's written to say he's throwing up his job with the family business and coming to London to try and get a job on the stage."

"Yes, he must be crazy to do such a thing!" Jenny put the dish on the table, then began to serve the meal.

"Come and have something to eat," she called, for Madge had not moved. "You'll feel better when you've eaten."

But Madge apparently had not heard her. Going to the little desk in the corner she took out a pad of notepaper and started to write.

"There!" she said at last, throwing her pen down and reading through what she had written. "I've told him exactly what I think about his plans. If he comes to London when he's read this, he'll at least know what I believe his chances of success are."

19

Jenny began to pile savoury fish pie on to a plate. "Now that you've got that out of your system, you'd better come and eat something!" she said.

A few minutes later she suddenly said: "How do you know that Jim isn't likely to be a success? He may be very good."

Madge frowned. "I'm sure he isn't, Jenny. I've seen him in amateur productions, and he's been — well adequate, but nothing more."

Jenny shrugged. "Oh, well, if he believes in himself, that's something these days, I suppose," she said. "At any rate, he can always go home to the family business if he's a failure."

Madge said nothing. She knew how high-spirited Jim was. To come to London full of hope, and then to have to admit failure, would be difficult for someone with Jim's temperament!

2

THE following morning, Miles sent Madge along to the wig department.

Madge found the different departments of the huge television organization fascinating. The props department, for instance, was a huge hall filled entirely with what at first sight appeared to be a bewildering array of junk. Yet here could be found, within minutes almost, any item that could possibly be needed. There were whole departments devoted entirely to historical costumes, to armour, to fire-arms, and to furniture — both antique and modern.

These various departments were housed in a dozen buildings that lay behind the main studios. A plan had been hung in the entrance hall of the administrative block to direct people to the particular department they wanted.

The wig department was a couple of rooms on the second floor at the back of the timber and joinery shop. Madge memorized the way she must go and, after one or two wrong turnings, eventually found herself climbing a narrow flight of stairs to a door at the top which was boldly marked: *Wig Department (Miss Ida Munro)*.

Madge knocked, and when a voice called: "Come in!" she pushed open the door and went into the narrow room beyond.

There were wigs everywhere, of varying colours, lengths and styles. Madge stared, fascinated, about her.

"What can I do for you, dear?"

Madge saw a little woman sitting on a low stool near the window, her long, sensitive fingers busy with a hank of hair. "I'm Mr. Brent's secretary," she said, as she went forward. "He wants to know if Mr. Weston's wig is ready."

"Yes. I have it over there."

The little woman stood up. She was very short and, as she went past

Madge, she limped painfully.

"Here it is." She turned back, holding the sleek, flaxen wig at armslength. "Isn't it lovely?"

"Did you make it?" Madge asked curiously.

The little woman nodded proudly. "Yes, I make many of the wigs that go out of here," she said.

Madge smiled. "I suppose there is a tremendous amount of work involved?"

"Oh, there is, I do assure you!"

"But you do have some help?"

"Oh, yes, I have some very good assistants. They're in there!" The little woman nodded towards an adjoining room.

Seeing that Madge was deeply interested, she led her back to the stool near the window and, for the next quarter of an hour, explained how she designed the wigs that were wanted for the productions; how she went through her stocks of human and animal hair, assessing how much would be needed; how she cut it to length and finally either completed the wig herself or handed it over to one of her assistants.

Madge suddenly glanced at her watch and, realizing that she had been there far too long, started back to the administrative block.

When she got to the bottom of the narrow staircase she was not quite sure whether she ought to turn to the right or to the left.

She hesitated. Should she go back to the wig department and ask the way? No, that was unnecessary. She was sure that the passage on the left was the one she had come along, and she set off in that direction.

Presently, she came to a door. Passing through this, she found herself in a very high-ceilinged store-room. It was almost full of scenery, which depicted every possible background. As Madge, intending to cross to the far side of this vast depository, went along the stacks of scenery, she saw flats of public buildings, churches, inns, and houses.

She came presently to the far wall. This had neither door nor window. The only light came into the storeroom from a big pane of glass set in the roof.

She decided to retrace her steps and return to the wig department. She should have done that in the first place. What a pity it was that there was no one in charge of the scenery who could have directed her.

But to her dismay, although she was sure she went back the way she had come, she did not find the door which had admitted her earlier.

She decided she must have gone down the wrong aisle between the rows of scenery. She had better start again.

At last she found herself wandering along a passageway with scenery depicting park railings and trees on one side and Grecian pillars on the other. Feeling much as Alice must have done when discovering Wonderland, she began to wonder if she was doomed to spend the rest of her life wandering amongst the maze of scenery.

"Is there anyone here?" she cried in sudden panic and, when there was no reply, she repeated the question more loudly.

Then, to her relief, a young man appeared at the end of the aisle. "Hello, are you lost?" he asked.

"Yes! I don't seem able to find the door."

He grinned. He had very white teeth and attractive wrinkles at the corners of his dark blue eyes. He was familiar to her, but she couldn't remember where she had seen him.

"Let's find the door together," he said in his deep voice, which had a gay lilt to it.

He took her arm and guided her along one line of scenery and down another.

"Here we are!" he said at last. "When you go through the door, you follow your nose until you come to a cobbled yard. Cross that, and I think you'll find yourself in familiar territory."

"Thank you, Mr. — ?" she began.

He grinned again. "Terry Black," he said and, turning on his heel, disappeared into the scenery department again.

As Madge went on her way, she found herself wondering how she had possibly failed to recognize Terry Black. He was acknowledged as one of the greatest entertainers on television; a man who could sing, dance, act and mimic, and do all four things equally well. How Miles Brent would laugh when she told him she had bumped into Terry Black and had not known him. Thinking of Miles made her realize that he must be wondering where on earth she had got to, and she almost ran back to the office.

However, when she arrived back, Miles was in a state about a crisis concerning one of the future productions, and her meeting with Terry Black completely slipped her mind, as she furiously typed and answered the constantly ringing telephone.

Altogether, it had been an exhausting day and, at the end of it, Madge felt fit for nothing except going straight to bed.

As she went wearily up the long flight of steps to the flat she found herself thinking, a little wistfully, of life as it had been back at home, in Hunsworth.

By this time, she would have been home quite two hours from the factory. High tea would be over, and she might be getting ready to go out for the evening with Jim — perhaps to the cinema or to a local dance. It had been a simple, uncomplicated way of life and, although she knew she really preferred the hectic rush and bustle of life at the TV studios, just occasionally — specially when she felt tired out — she thought, rather longingly of her mother and the pleasantly uneventful life she had once enjoyed in the north.

The flat was in darkness when she

let herself in. Perhaps, for once, Jenny, too, had had to work late.

With a heavy sigh of weariness, Madge switched on the lights and the electric fire, then went into the tiny kitchen to see what there was for supper. She was too tired to bother with anything elaborate, so decided to make do with frying herself some bacon and eggs.

As she stood watching the eggs sizzling in the pan, her mind once more went back to her home town. Jim should receive her letter tomorrow. He would be a fool to throw away a secure future in his father's business for the uncertainties of a career in the theatre.

She wondered how he would react to her letter. If he had any sense he would take her advice, but she knew Jim. He was headstrong and self-willed, and he would, perhaps, be resentful that she had presumed to advise him.

As she was about to lift the eggs out of the pan, the doorbell rang. She sighed in exasperation. No doubt Jenny had forgotten her key again! Tonight she was in the sort of mood when anything could annoy her and, feeling irritated out of all proportion, she went to the front door.

"I'm just getting a meal ready — !" she said, as she opened the door.

Then, mouth open, she stared in amazement, at the tall, smiling young man who stood on the landing outside.

"Hello, darling!" he cried and, moving forward, took her in his arms.

After he had hugged her, he held her at armslength and looked at her appreciatively. "I told you I was coming to London!" he cried. "I didn't waste much time, did I?"

"But, Jim!" she gasped, trying to convince herself that it really was Jim Lingard standing before her and not a figment of her imagination. "I — I wrote to you when I got your letter. I — I said . . . "

"How glad you would be to see me when I arrived, eh?" he laughed; then, releasing her, he bent to pick up the suitcase by his side and moved past her into the sitting-room.

"I've been travelling since lunch-time," he said. "And I'm as hungry as a hunter."

He sniffed appreciatively and Madge, because there seemed nothing else she could do, closed the door.

3

"IT's wonderful to see you again, Madge!"

Jim Lingard crossed to Madge's side and slipped his arm about her slim waist. "So this is the wonderful flat I've heard so much about," he said, looking around him. "Where's Jenny?"

"She's not come in yet. She should be home any minute."

He looked down at her with an affectionate smile that lit up his rather plain face and set his grey eyes twinkling. "You haven't given me a kiss yet," he said. "I — "

"The bacon's burning!" Madge exclaimed, and twisted away from him. She hurried across the room and Jim stared after her, a little frown on his face.

This wasn't the rapturous meeting he had imagined he would get when he

32

turned up at Madge's flat. He found her coolness unaccountable. Was it something to do with the letter she had mentioned?

"Could I have a wash?" he asked, going to the door of the tiny kitchen.

Madge looked round from the stove. "The bathroom's down the passage," she said. "Supper will be ready when you come back. You'd better eat Jenny's share, as she isn't here, and I'll do some more when she arrives."

Madge bit her lip as Jim turned away from her. Why was she behaving like this towards him? Though they were not officially engaged, both had taken it for granted that they would get married some day. Yet she had treated him as if he was little more than a stranger who had turned up at an inconvenient time.

When he came back from the bathroom she linked her arm through his and led him to the table.

"Sit here," she said — and, as he sat before the plate of bacon and eggs, she

33

dropped a kiss on his unruly shock of fair hair.

The puzzled frown disappeared from Jim's face and he grinned in relief. "That's better," he declared. "Just for a moment, you had me worried! I thought you weren't glad to see me."

"Of course I'm glad to see you!" She put down her own plate and sat beside him. "It's just that — well, when I read your letter I wrote back to say I thought you were making a mistake, throwing everything up in Hunsworth and coming to London to try your luck in the theatre."

He frowned. "But, Madge, surely you didn't think I'd do a thing like that without being pretty sure that I'd something to come to!"

Her face lit up. "You mean, you've got a job?"

For a moment or two he did not speak, then he said slowly: "No, I haven't actually got a job — yet. But don't worry, I won't be out of work for long. I know a very good agent."

He told her how, whilst appearing in an amateur production in Hunsworth, a London theatrical agent, staying in the district on business, had attended the show.

"He came round to the dressing-room afterwards, Madge," Jim cried in sudden excitement. "He said he had been very impressed by my performance and that if I ever came to London I was to be sure to call on him. He gave me his card."

He fetched out his wallet and produced the card. Madge's heart sank as she read the name of a theatrical agent she had often heard Miles Brent speak of with contempt.

"Charges people a large fee and makes out they're all Henry Irvings," Miles had said. "Of course, he rarely gets them any work. All he's in the game for is to squeeze them dry while he pretends to find them a job."

"Well, have you heard of him?" Jim demanded, when she did not speak.

She forced a smile and nodded. "Yes, I've heard of him, Jim," she said. "There are quite a lot of theatrical agents like him in London. He may or may not get you a job. It depends."

He scowled. His lower lip protruded obstinately.

"I think you're trying to put me off, Madge," he muttered. "Mr. Leslie seemed quite impressed by my work. I'm hoping to see him tomorrow."

"Well, good luck!" she said, trying to sound sincere. Then she heard Jenny's key in the lock.

Jim and Jenny, of course, had met in Hunsworth many times before, and they greeted each other with delight.

"So you decided to find out if the streets of London really are paved with gold!" Jenny cried.

"I'm prepared to be disappointed," Jim grinned; then, looking at Madge: "I've a feeling Madge believes I'd have done better to stay at home."

"Only for your own sake!" Madge cried. "I don't want you to build too much hope on this agent you're going to see."

Jenny glancing from one to the other, decided to change the subject. "I hope you enjoyed my supper," she said with a twinkle, eyeing Jim's empty plate.

"I'll cook you some more," Madge said quickly before Jim could reply, and hurried into the kitchen, leaving her two friends together.

She felt within her the need to protect Jim from disappointment and disillusionment, yet she knew that he would take little notice of her warnings. Perhaps he would listen to a man more attentively. Perhaps she could get Miles Brent to speak to him. If Jim had any sense he would take heed of a man who had had such wide experience in the theatrical and television world.

But Madge did not broach the subject again that evening. Instead, she, Jim and Jenny spent a couple of pleasant hours, exchanging news and gossip.

Soon it was ten o'clock and Madge looked inquiringly at Jim. "By the way,

Jim, where are you staying tonight?" she asked.

He looked slightly embarrassed. "As a matter of fact, I haven't booked in at an hotel yet," he said. "I meant to go on my way as soon as I had called to see you, but — well, there seems to have been so much to talk about . . ."

"Why don't you stay here?" Jenny asked. "There are two bedrooms. You can have mine and I'll double up with Madge for tonight. There's a double bed in her room."

"Oh, I couldn't possibly put you to all that trouble," Jim protested.

Jenny went to the window and pulled the curtain aside. "It's raining," she said. "You'd be wise to accept our offer, my lad. It will be most unpleasant traipsing the streets looking for a hotel on a night like this."

"Well, thanks," Jim said gratefully. "Is it all right with you, Madge?"

"Of course it is!" she cried. "I'll go and change the bed now."

Later, when Jenny had tactfully gone to the bathroom to brush her teeth, Jim held her close. "It's wonderful being here in London with you, Madge," he said, and fiercely: "I mean to make a go of things. You do believe that, don't you?"

"Of course I do, Jim," she whispered, giving him a hug. "If I didn't seem as enthusiastic as I might have done when you arrived, it was because I care very much what happens to you. I know enough about show business now to realize that one has a pretty rough time getting to the top."

"You think I mightn't make a go of it, is that it?" He was on the defensive again.

She slipped her arms round his neck and stood on tiptoe to kiss him. "All I want is for you not to be hurt," she said gently; then, because she could hear Jenny coming back, she slipped out of the circle of his arms and went into her bedroom.

Although it had been a long and

eventful day, Madge found it hard to sleep. She lay beside Jenny, staring into the darkness.

"Jim's taking a big chance in leaving Hunsworth, I hope he isn't going to be disappointed," Jenny said suddenly.

"Oh, I thought you were asleep, Jenny," Madge exclaimed, then added remorsefully: "I didn't tell Jim so, but Mr. Brent knows this agent, Mr. Leslie. Evidently, he's not got too good a reputation in the business."

"I don't think I'd mention that to Jim," Jenny advised. "He seems to me to be the sort of person who'd rather find things out for himself."

"Yes, it's difficult to tell Jim any-thing. He's so headstrong."

"Let him try, then. If he fails, he will have no one to blame but himself. If the worst comes to the worst he can always go back into the family business."

"Yes, I suppose you're right. But I can't help feeling that Jim will take it very badly if he is disappointed."

★ ★ ★

Madge spent a restless night and, because she felt that no good would come of lying in bed any longer, she was up much earlier than Jim or Jenny. Jim appeared, looking fresh-eyed and spruce.

"Are you seeing Mr. Leslie today?" Madge asked.

"Yes. The sooner I see what sort of a job he can offer me, the better."

It was on the tip of her tongue to tell him what Miles had said about the agent, but Jenny came rushing into the room like a tornado. Jim would not like her warning him, anyway, and to do so in front of Jenny would be unforgivable.

"I suppose I'd better find a room," Jim said when, after drinking a cup of tea and eating a slice of toast, Madge said she must dash, or she'd be late.

"You can stay on here for the time being, if you like," Jenny said. "Can't he, Madge?"

"Yes, of course, if you don't mind," Madge replied.

"That's jolly decent of you both," Jim said gratefully. "Then, if it's all the same to you, I'll concentrate on trying to get a job today and look round for digs later."

Madge sat on the bus, going to the office, wishing she didn't feel so apprehensive about Jim's future in London. After all, he was the man she was supposed to be marrying and she should have had faith in him — the same sort of faith that he had in himself.

That morning, Miles Brent found Madge not to be the efficient, attentive secretary she usually was. More than once she had to ask him, when he was dictating letters, to repeat what he had said.

At last, when he asked her to read some of her shorthand back, and she was unable to do so, he frowned across the desk at her. "What on earth's the matter this morning, Madge?" he demanded. "Aren't you feeling well?"

"I'm fine!" she said, angry with herself for allowing her concern for Jim to interfere with her work.

"Then, what's come over you? You're not usually like this."

Meeting his puzzled gaze she suddenly found herself overcome with an urgent desire to confide in him. "Mr. Brent, I . . . " she began, but he shook his head with a smile.

"Couldn't you bring yourself to call me 'Miles'?" he asked. "Everybody else does, you know."

She forced a smile. "Thanks Miles. I'm sorry I've made so many mistakes this morning. I've got something on my mind."

"If it would help to tell me about it, fire away!" he said, sitting back in his chair, and studying her face intently.

She told him, then, about Jim turning up and about the agent he was going to see that day.

"I remember what you said about this Mr. Leslie, the agent," she said.

"I just cannot bear to think about Jim being taken in like that."

Miles stood up and went over to the window.

Madge sat, looking at his back, and almost wishing that she had not told him about Jim. It had been rather presumptuous of her to imagine that he, one of the best known figures in the television world, should find her small, personal problems of any possible interest.

However, after a short silence, Miles turned around to face her again. "I take it that you're in love with this young man?" he asked.

She felt the colour coming into her face. "I — I suppose I am," she admitted. "Before I came to London we had discussed getting married, one day."

He nodded. "Why don't you send him along to see me? I might even arrange for him to have a test. If he's good enough, it could lead to a part. Who knows?"

44

"It's very good of you," she said. "I don't want any favours for Jim, just because I'm your secretary."

He shrugged. "Don't feel guilty on that account, Madge. As you know, we're producing plays in this department every week and we could use a few decent young actors. If he is good, then I shall have everything to gain, and if he's not — well, I shan't lose anything by it."

"I don't know what to say!" Madge said.

"Then don't say it! Let's get back to the letters. Now your mind's more at rest, perhaps you'll be able to read your shorthand back to me!"

When Madge got back to the flat, that evening, Jim and Jenny were already there. Jenny was busily preparing the supper, and Jim was sitting, staring rather morosely into the red glow of the electric fire. "Hello, Madge!" he said. "Had a good day?"

"A tiring one, but not too bad on the whole," she said, taking off her

45

coat. "How about you? Did you see Mr. Leslie?"

He nodded. "Yes, I saw him. He was a very different man from the one I met in Hunsworth."

Madge heard the bitter note in his voice. So his disillusionment had started already, had it?

"Did he offer you a part of any sort?" she asked.

He shook his head angrily. "No, all he seemed to want to do was to make me pay a large fee for enrolling. He said, before he could do anything for me, I had to register on his books."

"And you paid up?"

"What else could I do? When I'd handed the money over, I reminded him of his visit to Hunsworth and how he'd said there would be little difficulty in placing me in some production. He laughed in my face."

"Poor Jim!" Madge said, fighting back a sudden desire to say, "I told you so." Jim looked so upset that she hadn't the heart. Instead, she put her hand on his arm. "Jim, I've got news for you," she said quietly. "I spoke to Mr. Brent about you this morning. He says he'd like to see you. At any rate even if he doesn't offer you a part, he can advise you about television work and the opportunities that might occur for you."

At her words Jim's eyes lit up. "That's very decent of you, Madge. You mean Miles Brent, your boss, don't you?"

"Yes, he's a producer, and a very important man."

"I know he's quite a big shot with MTV. It would be a wonderful start if I could get a part in one of his shows."

"Don't build on it too much, Jim — " Madge began, but Jim's spirits had soared, and he was not listening to her. Instead, he seized her in his arms and waltzed her around the room. Jenny, coming into the room with a tureen of vegetables, stared in amazement. "What's got into you!" she cried. "The last time I saw you, Jim, you were staring moodily into space, as if you were contemplating suicide."

"I'm suicidal no longer, Jenny," he cried, hugging Madge close. "I'm to see the great man himself — Mr. Miles Brent — in person."

"Good for you! You'll like him," Jenny said, and went back to the kitchen for the chops she had been cooking.

Jim looked down at Madge with a frown. "Has Jenny met Mr. Brent?" he asked.

For some reason Madge felt uneasy. "He brought me home the other evening and came in for a drink," she said, and added lamely: "He's very nice."

Jenny — who had overhead this, called out: 'Very nice,' she says! Why, Jim, he's fabulous — much too good for that awful girl he's engaged to! What's her name, Madge? Patricia Carnford, isn't it?"

Madge felt the tense arm round her

waist relax. Jim was smiling again. "Oh, he's engaged, is he? I suppose all these television types tend to marry people in the same line of business."

He smiled down at Madge. "When can I see him, love? Will you make an appointment, or shall I?"

"I'll do it," she said and, as she went with Jim to the table, she fiercely suppressed the disloyal thought that perhaps he had been expecting her to use her influence with Miles Brent to help him to get a job.

4

DURING supper, Jim looked across at the two girls with shining eyes. "You've both been wonderful to me since I came to London," he said. "I'd like to do something for you both, in return."

Jenny smiled across the table at him. "Such as?" she asked.

"Well, let's go out after supper. We can take a cab to the West End and find a night club."

"Night clubs cost money, my lad," Jenny said. "Don't forget — you're an unemployed actor now, not a printing tycoon."

He grinned. "Don't worry about that. I've still got a pound or two to spare. When I'm approaching bankruptcy, I'll let you know." He glanced at Madge. "Well, what do you say?"

Madge felt her usual weariness after

a long day at the office and wanted nothing more than to put her feet up in front of the fire. But she forced a smile. She knew Jim well enough to be quite sure that he had set his heart on this outing to the West End.

"It sounds fun," she said.

"Marvellous!" Jim cried. "Where shall we go? I'm afraid I don't know much about the night life of London."

"What makes you think we know any more than you?" Jenny demanded. "Madge and I haven't exactly lived a life of hectic gaiety since we came to London."

Madge nodded. "That's true enough, Jim. We're usually too tired or I'm too late home to go much farther than the cinema."

He laughed. "Well, now that I am here, things will change. I may only be a Yorkshire lad, but I know how to have a good time. Right, I'm raring to go, so let's get cracking!"

They consulted the evening paper Jim

had brought in with him earlier in the evening. Several late-night restaurants with dancing were advertised, and they decided to go to the *Candlelight Bar* first.

"After that, we'll let instinct guide us!" Jim cried. "And now, ladies, put on your finery and let us away!"

They departed in a taxi Jim had summoned by telephone. As they drove through the lamp-lit streets, Madge felt excitement rising within her. She felt Jim's hand close over hers. He was sitting between the two girls at the back of the taxi. "Happy?" he whispered, turning towards her.

She nodded, eyes shining. Yes, she really was happy. For the first time since Jim had turned up so unexpectedly she was prepared to stop worrying and just enjoy herself.

The *Candlelight Bar* turned out to be a small basement club, with whitewashed walls and attractive Spanish décor. The room was lit by candles, and these cast on to the pale wall the flickering shadows of the few couples who danced in the centre of the floor.

Jim and the two girls were settled at a table, and Jim ordered a bottle of sherry. Then he stood up and said that he wanted to dance. "Dance with Jenny first," Madge said, because she did not want her friend to feel the odd one out in the trio. However, just for a moment, Madge felt an unreasonable stab of jealousy as she watched Jim and Jenny in one another's arms. They were laughing heartily about something. Jenny seemed almost more at ease with Jim than she did herself.

Seconds later, she was telling herself not to be a fool. Jenny got on with everyone. She had such a sense of fun that she was popular wherever she went.

"When do you think I'll be able to see Miles Brent?" Jim asked, when he was dancing with Madge.

"I'll try to fix an appointment," she promised.

"I'd like to see him as soon as

possible," he said. "It's not much fun kicking one's heels in London with nothing to do."

It was on the tip of Madge's tongue to warn him that there might be many days in the next few weeks when he would have little to do, but she restrained herself. There was no point in depressing Jim.

"I'll speak to him tomorrow," she said, and he gave her a grateful little squeeze.

"Now, how about going on to *The Painted Cloud* club? There's a cabaret there at midnight."

"Okay," Madge agreed. "Let's do that. That is, if you're sure you can afford it, Jim. You're not really in a position to throw money away."

"Stop worrying," Jim said affectionately. "You really are an old fuss-pot, Madge."

Jenny was entirely in agreement that they should all go on to *The Painted Cloud*, and very shortly Jim summoned another taxi, and they were once more driving through the brightly lit streets of the West End.

The Painted Cloud was much more elaborate and formal than the *Candlelight Bar*. A rather supercilious head waiter greeted Jim, Jenny and Madge and, after consulting a list, announced that he was sorry but he hadn't a table for three.

"Surely you can squeeze us in somewhere, old chap?" Jim said persuasively.

The head waiter looked at him, haughtily. "The cabaret is due to start in a quarter of an hour, sir," he said. "I might have managed something if you had arrived a few minutes earlier than this."

Jim seemed inclined to argue, but Madge took his arm. "We can go somewhere else, Jim," she whispered, then gave a sudden start as a familiar voice said: "Hello, Madge! What are you doing here?"

Madge swung round and saw Miles Brent, accompanied by Patricia Carnford. They had evidently just arrived.

The head waiter obviously knew Miles, and was beaming at him. "Good evening, Mr. Brent! Good evening, Miss Carnford!" he gushed. "I have your table all ready for you, sir."

Miles ignored him. "Is Jules being difficult?" he asked Madge.

"There isn't a table," she replied, feeling very uncomfortable under Patricia Carnford's cold stare. "We were just going."

"Nonsense!" Miles turned to the head waiter. "If there isn't a table for them, they can sit at mine, Jules."

The man hesitated, then snapped his fingers to summon another waiter over. Orders were given, extra chairs were fetched, and soon the entire party was seated at a table near the edge of the dance floor.

"You should have a good view of the cabaret from here," Miles said, smiling at Madge. "And now, how about some introductions?"

Madge murmured Jim's and Jenny's names and Patricia nodded formally and unsmilingly. She was not making any attempt to conceal her displeasure at the appearance of Madge and her friends.

Miles shook Jim's hand warmly. "Madge told me about you," he said. "Perhaps you would like to come along to the studio and see me. I might be able to fix you up, if you're any good."

"That's very kind of you," Jim smiled. "The sooner the better, as far as I'm concerned."

"Then make it tomorrow afternoon about four. Okay?"

"Marvellous! I'll be there on the dot."

Miles and Patricia were having a meal, and Jim insisted upon paying for the wine.

"We're imposing ourselves upon you," he said. "It's the least I can do."

Madge studied Miles discreetly. At first she had had the impression that he had felt obliged to offer her and her friends a place at his table, but now she began to believe that he was genuinely pleased to have them there — grateful, almost, that he was not to be alone with Patricia. She wondered if he and his fiancée had quarrelled; she looked so cold and angry, and not the flicker of a smile crossed her face, not even when the cabaret began and the others were roaring at the wisecracks of a famous comedian.

When the cabaret was over, Madge was surprised to hear Miles asking her to dance. She hesitated. Surely he ought to dance with Patricia first? However, Patricia had already been appropriated by Jim, who was leading her to the centre of the floor.

"Don't look so worried, Madge," Miles chided her, as they moved round the floor in a slow waltz.

"It seems so awful, crashing in on you and Miss Carnford," she said, shyly.

"Nonsense! Pat doesn't mind, and neither do I. So just concentrate on enjoying yourself. By the way, I like your fiancé. I hope I'll be able to help him."

Madge longed to tell him that Jim was not her fiancé — not officially — but that somehow seemed disloyal to Jim, who obviously expected her to marry him some day.

"It's very kind of you to take so much interest in him," she said as the music stopped and they returned to their table.

"I'll look forward to talking to him when he comes to the studio," Miles told her. He asked Jenny for the next dance, and Madge sat alone at the table, for Patricia was still clasped in Jim's arms, and they seemed to be in earnest conversation. Later on, when Jim and Madge were dancing together, she asked him how he had got on with Patricia.

"Very well," he replied. "I told her that she was my favourite TV star and that seemed to please her."

I'll bet it did! Madge thought.

Patricia was the sort of girl who would lap up any flattery.

"She thinks I'll do well on television," Jim went on. "She says she's going to try to use her influence with Miles to get me a job. And if he's not very helpful — well, she knows lots of other people who could be useful to me."

Madge felt a twinge of misgiving. Surely Jim must see that, if he was to succeed, he must do so without too much help from other people. But she did not say anything. Obviously, Jim was feeling very pleased with himself tonight. She would only annoy him if she tried to daunt his high spirits.

It was two o'clock before Patricia Carnford suddenly announced that she was tired and wanted Miles to take her home.

It was a signal for the party to end. While the girls collected their coats, Miles and Jim waited for them in the entrance hall.

"Madge tells me you left your father's

business to come to London," Miles said. "Printing, isn't it?"

"Yes! It's quite a good little business, but — well, it isn't exactly what I want to do with my life."

"I don't suppose it seems as romantic as a career on the stage," Miles said. "But it might prove far more rewarding in the end."

"Are you trying to put me off acting, before I've even had a chance to prove myself?" Jim said, lightly.

"Far from it! There is a shortage of good young actors at the moment. Ah, here are the girls! Have you a car, by the way?"

"No," Jim said. "I'll ask the doorman to get us a taxi."

"Nothing of the kind. My old bus is big enough for five. Follow me!"

They went out into the quiet street. Miles's roomy old car was parked near by. "I'll run you people home first," he said.

Madge glanced at Patricia's face and saw that her lips were pursed in anger.

61

"I'm sure we could get a taxi," she said quickly, and looked at Jenny and Jim for support.

"Nonsense! I won't hear of it. Jump in!" Miles demanded.

"I really am awfully tired, darling — " Patricia murmured, but already the others had been ushered into the back seat, and Miles was holding open the door for her to seat herself beside him.

The short journey through the quiet streets took only twenty minutes. "See you tomorrow at four, then," Miles said, as Jim and the two girls left the car.

Jim nodded; then, as Miles and Patricia drove away, he took Madge and Jenny by the arm.

"I feel I shall sleep until midday," he said, as they went into the house.

"You're lucky!" Jenny said tartly. "Unfortunately, I have to be at the office by half past nine at the latest."

"So have I!" Madge murmured.

"Then hurry into bed and I'll bring

you a nice hot drink," he said, as Madge opened the door of the flat.

They did not take him seriously but, twenty minutes later, when they were getting ready for bed, there was a knock at the door. Jenny slipped on her dressing-gown, and went out on to the landing. Jim stood there with two mugs of steaming cocoa.

"He's rather sweet, isn't he?" Jenny said, as she sat on the bed, sipping her drink. He'll make a wonderful husband when he gets all these ideas of being an actor out of his system!"

"Nobody seems to have any faith in Jim's ability," Madge said suddenly. "Not even me, and I should have the utmost confidence in him."

Jenny shrugged. "Well, if I were going to marry him, I'd want to be sure he knew exactly what he was doing about the future!"

"Jenny — " Madge said, about to confide to her friend that she wasn't sure that she ever would be married to Jim, but Jenny had wriggled under the bedclothes and was no longer listening.

* * *

In the morning, Madge saw little of Miles Brent. With a new production nearing completion he was here, there and everywhere, discussing points with the dramatist, the designer of the sets, the camera crews, the lighting men . . .

When he came into the office before lunch Madge thought he looked harassed and unhappy and she wondered if Patricia Carnford had proved difficult on the previous night, after he had dropped them off.

"What have I got to do this afternoon?" he demanded, standing before her desk, a frown on his rather solemn face.

"You've a rehearsal at two and Mr. Holman asked if you'd give him a few minutes to discuss the script for *The Man In The Chair*," Madge replied. "Then, my friend, Jim Lingard, is coming in at four."

"Oh, yes." The frown deepened. "He may have to wait a bit, if Holman keeps me a long time."

"Would you rather I put him off and asked him to come in another day?"

"No, don't do that! As a matter of fact, I've a particular reason for wanting to see him."

She must have seemed startled by this for suddenly he smiled, a smile which chased the frown from his face. "I haven't time to explain now," he said. "I'm having lunch with Toby Pateley. See you later!" He was gone and she was left wondering what particular reason he could possibly have for wanting to see Jim.

The afternoon seemed to drag. Miles had said he could manage without Madge at the rehearsal and she filled in the time by typing some letters he had dictated, the previous afternoon.

At last four o'clock came and, simultaneously with the chiming of a near-by church clock, Jim entered the office, escorted by a messenger boy.

"Where's Mr. Brent?" he asked, when the messenger had departed.

"He'll be along soon," Madge told him. "He had to see one of the scriptwriters after the rehearsal and he hasn't come back yet. How do you feel after your late night?"

"I didn't get up till eleven o'clock," Jim said, sinking into a chair. "I didn't wake up until half-past ten. Well, if I had been awake I would only have been worrying about this afternoon."

The door opened and Miles came into the office. He smiled at Jim as they shook hands. "Sorry to keep you waiting, old man," he said. "Sit down, and we'll talk things over."

Madge, sent out for two cups of tea by Miles, returned presently to hear the producer say: "So you'll have to have a test as soon as it can be arranged. Tomorrow, I hope!"

Jim's eyes were shining. He's very pleased about something, Madge thought, as he took the cup she held out.

"And you really think you can put me into Friday's episode of *The Carruthers Family*?" Jim asked.

"If the test shows you have any ability at all," Miles replied. "It's an ill wind that blows nobody any good, so you can thank Alan Baxter for walking out on me at the last minute. It isn't a big part — in fact, you'll only have half a dozen lines to learn — but it's a start."

Madge's heart quickened. *The Carruthers Family* was a twice-weekly series and, although it demanded little of an actor, it was as good a beginning as any. Many people, she knew, had been spotted and given more important parts after an appearance in this show.

And if Jim was as good as he thought he was, perhaps he really would make good.

She shook herself out of her reverie, as Miles stood up. "And now I'm pretty busy," he said. "I'll get Madge to fix the test. She can tell you this evening what time you've to report."

Madge went out of the office with Jim and, as the door closed behind them, Jim gave her a quick kiss. "I've you to thank for this," he said delightedly. "You're a wonderful girl!"

He gave her another kiss, then hurried away along the long corridor. Madge watched him out of sight, and then, with a little sigh, she turned and went back into the office. She wished, for Jim's sake, that she could feel more enthusiastic than she did.

5

JIM was so elated that he decided to get off the bus a few stops earlier than he normally did, and walk the rest of the way. Only by strenuous exercise would he be able to subdue the excitement that had gripped him ever since Miles Brent had spoken of giving him a part in the television serial.

Now he was on his way up. In a few months — perhaps even a few weeks — his face would be as familiar to the public as were other well-known television personalities.

As he strode along a quiet street of Victorian houses a notice hanging in one of the windows, declaring that there was a flat to let, caught his attention.

It occurred to him, not for the first time, that he must not impose upon Madge's and Jenny's hospitality for much longer. After all, they were suffering a certain amount of inconvenience on his account and it was up to him to get a flat of his own as soon as possible.

On impulse, he went up the short flight of stone steps and rang the doorbell labelled *Housekeeper*.

Presently, the door was opened by a rather formidable, middle-aged woman with greying hair. "Yes?" she said, roughly.

"You have a flat to let," he said, indicating the card in the window.

"Yes!" Her eyes took in his smart suit, his generally presentable appearance. Evidently he passed the test, for she stepped back and invited him to enter.

"It's on the top floor," she told him, as they went along the dark hall and started to climb a narrow flight of stairs. "Just the one room with a kitchen. You share the bathroom, which is on the floor below."

To Jim, used to his parents' rambling old house on the outskirts of Hunsworth, the accommodation seemed very limiting. However, he suspended judgment until they were standing in the middle of the sitting-room, which was obviously a converted attic-room. The furniture was old but substantial-looking and the carpet was badly worn. The kitchen, which was really little more than a curtained alcove, contained gas-ring and sink. Jim peered out of the grimy kitchen window. What a depressing view to greet one every day — just grey chimney pot after grey chimney pot.

"The room was only vacated yesterday," the lady — who had introduced herself as Mrs. Fisher-Smith — declared. "I think you'd be well advised to decide here and now, if you want it, Mr. Lingard."

"I'd like to think it over," Jim said. "Perhaps I could let you know in the morning. Are you on the telephone?"

Rather reluctantly, the woman gave him the number and led him downstairs again.

Jim was glad to be in the fresh air again. There had been such a dank, musty smell about the house. Still, he supposed it would do, for the time being. He wished that Madge had been there to advise him.

When he got in he was surprised to find Jenny in the kitchen, making herself a cup of tea, although it was only just five o'clock.

"My boss has gone to Paris," she said. "She let me come home early. Said there was no point in sticking around, if she wasn't there. Have a cup of tea."

He told her, as they sat before the fire, sipping their tea, how he might get a part in an episode of *The Carruthers Family*. "Apparently, what is needed is a genuine Yorkshire accent," Jim said, grinning. "Isn't it amazing? I thought my accent would severely impede my acting career, but Miles Brent says there's a shortage of young actors, with a natural knowledge of local dialects. Anyway, if I get the job, I'm to play

Archie Carruther's Yorkshire cousin, up to town for the weekend. What a bit of luck that the actor, signed up to play the lad, walked out on Mr. Brent because of a money dispute. Money dispute! I tell you, lass, I'd do this part for nothing!"

"Oh, it's wonderful, Jim," Jenny cried. "I used to watch *The Carruthers Family* regularly, when I lived at home. It should be great fun!" Jim watched her beaming face and thought, with a pang that she was being far more enthusiastic than Madge had been.

"I'll have to get a flat, now I've the possibility of a job," Jim said. "I can't impose on you and Madge any longer."

"Stay as long as you like," Jenny said. "We like having a man around to bully!"

"I had a look at a place on my way back. I don't know whether to take it or not. I think a woman could weigh it up better than a man."

"I'm sure Madge will go round to see it with you."

"I may lose it if I leave it too long. I have to let the woman know tomorrow morning at the latest. It's not very far away from here." He looked at her closely.

"It certainly is hard to get decent accommodation in London." Jenny hesitated, then said tentatively: "I'll come along with you, if you like, Jim. It will save Madge having to turn out again when she arrives home, dog tired."

His eyes shone. "Would you really, Jenny? You really are a brick. I'll just go and get my coat. We can catch a bus almost to the door."

A few minutes later, they were leaving the house. A taxi was coming along the street and Jim, on impulse, hailed it. As Jenny climbed in, she said over her shoulder: "You won't have to let one small part in a TV soap opera go to your head, my lad. Taxis are expensive luxuries, as you'll soon find out."

He grinned as he joined her on the back seat. "I don't find a new home every day of the week," he said. "If it will make you feel any better, we'll take a bus back."

Jenny saw a lace curtain move slightly as the taxi drew up outside Mrs. Fisher-Smith's house.

"So you've brought your young lady with you, have you?" the woman said to Jim, when she opened the door.

He frowned. "She's just a friend. I thought she would advise me about the room, if you don't mind letting us see it together."

"Certainly! You know where it is, Mr. Lingard. If you'll excuse me, I'll not climb all those stairs again. You will find me at the back of the house, when you come down."

She disappeared along the passage and Jim followed Jenny to the top of the house.

"This is it," he said, opening the door of the sitting-room.

Jenny did not speak for several minutes, as she gazed around the room. Then she swung round to Jim.

"And how much did you say she wanted for it?" she demanded.

Jim named a sum and Jenny's lips curled as she studied the ancient furniture and threadbare carpet. She went into the kitchen, examined it closely, and then asked: "Have you seen the bathroom yet?"

"No! I — I didn't think that was necessary. And she didn't suggest it."

She eyed him with scorn. "Men!" she exploded. "No wonder the price of rooms is so high in London. If people are willing to pay these prices, then obviously the landladies are going to get away with murder."

"What do you think of it?" Jim asked. "Not much, I suppose, if the expression on your face is anything to go by."

To his surprise, Jenny smiled. "When I first came to London I saw things that were a hundred times worse than this. This is no palace, but it's not bad, and I think you should take it; but not at the sum you mentioned. You must try to bargain with the old lady."

"Would it be right to do that?" Jim asked.

Jenny laughed. "Under that sophisticated exterior you really are an innocent abroad, aren't you? Never mind, leave Mrs. Fisher-Smith to me."

They went downstairs. The woman must have been lurking at the end of the passage for she came quickly forward, smiling broadly when they appeared.

"Have you decided?" she asked.

Before Jim could speak, Jenny said: "He's decided to take it, if you deduct thirty shillings from the suggested rent."

The woman drew herself up and clasped her hands across her ample bosom.

"I told Mr. Lingard — " she began, but Jenny interrupted her.

"I know very well what you told him, but you can hardly expect anyone to pay that price for such shabby accommodation."

"Well, I — " Mrs. Fisher-Smith

began, and then seemed lost for words.

"The handbasin is cracked," Jenny went on remorselessly. "The gas ring is rusty and there is a large hole in the living-room carpet. I looked in the bathroom as we came downstairs and — well, really, I thought that old type of geyser went out years ago. As for the linoleum, well — " Jenny paused, to allow her words to take effect.

The woman's face had reddened with anger, and Jim thought that she would probably throw Jenny and himself out of the door. Instead, she said in a suddenly ingratiating voice: "A great number of improvements are scheduled, but you know how difficult it is these days to find really good workmen. I like Mr. Lingard and, as a special concession, I will reduce the rent by thirty shillings. I wouldn't do this for anyone, mind, but I can see Mr. Lingard is a good type."

Jenny glanced at Jim, who was looking bewildered at the sudden change in Mrs. Fisher-Smith's manner. "Well, is that all right with you, Jim?"

"Yes," he said, "that will be fine."

A few minutes later, Jim and Jenny were walking along the road. "Gosh! I've never seen anything like it," Jim cried admiringly. "I didn't know you had it in you, Jenny."

She smiled rather slyly as she looked sideways at him. "There are lots of things you don't know about me, Jim," she murmured, then started to run: "There's a bus coming. If we miss it, we might wait ages for the next, and I've supper to cook before Madge gets home."

They arrived home just a few minutes before Madge, and the first thing she said as she came through the door was that Jim's test was fixed for ten o'clock the following morning.

"What shall I have to do?" he asked.

"Read some lines. Register fright, apprehension, happiness — oh, the usual thing."

"That doesn't sound very difficult!"

"Don't treat it too lightly, Jim," she warned. "I've seen quite a few people going for a test, believing it was childishly easy, and then finding they hadn't passed. I wouldn't like it to happen to you."

He grinned. "I hope it won't! But let's forget about the test for a minute, Madge. I've found somewhere to live."

Her eyes lit up. "How wonderful! Where is it?"

"It's a few minutes bus ride from here. It's not much of a room, but it'll do for the time being."

"I went along with him to make sure he didn't pay too much," Jenny said, coming into the sitting-room with a dish of chops she had just cooked.

"She saved me thirty shillings a week!" Jim chuckled. "You should have seen her, Madge, bullying the poor old landlady. I didn't know that Jenny could be so aggressive."

"Nonsense! I only stood up to her, as you should have done in the first place," Jenny said tartly. "Come and eat your supper, folks, before it gets cold."

Madge, listening to Jenny and Jim laughing at Mrs. Fisher-Smith's defeat, found herself feeling rather jealous. Surely she should have been the one to go along with Jim to look at the flat and see that he got the right sort of accommodation.

★ ★ ★

Jim went along to the studios with Madge in the morning. She delivered him to the make-up department, where he would be prepared for the screen test, then went up to the office she shared with Miles Brent. She found the producer searching for a script.

"I put it on my desk, yesterday evening," he said irritably. "Why does everything get moved round so much?"

She went to the filing cabinet. "I put the script away," she said. "You surely haven't forgotten how we lost that script after the cleaners had been in? I — "

"All right, all right!" He took the

script from her. "Has your young man gone to have his test?"

"Yes, I've just left him down there. They promised to let you see the rushes at twelve o'clock."

"Good! And if they're okay, he'd better attend the rehearsal this afternoon. There isn't too much time to fit him into Alan's part, small though it is."

The morning passed swiftly. Madge, in between typing, answering the telephone and taking messages from Miles, spared a thought for Jim taking his test.

More than once, she wondered what his reaction would be if he failed. He was so confident, and it was usually the over-confident who failed to come up to expectations.

Then suddenly the door opened and he was there. Miles had gone to a script conference and she was alone.

"Well, how did it go?" she asked.

He went to her side, pulled her to her feet and kissed her hard. "Easy as falling off a log!" he cried.

The door opened and Miles Brent came into the room. Madge, conscious that Jim was holding her close, drew away from him and Miles smiled. "Don't let me disturb you!" he said. "I take it the test is over?"

Jim grinned. "Yes, I was just telling Madge I thought it had gone quite well."

"We'll soon see," Miles declared. "You can both come down to the projection room and we'll all take a look at it. Ring and see if they're ready for us yet, Madge."

She went to the telephone, glad to have something to do to cover her embarrassment. Yet, as she spoke to the man in the projection room, she wondered why she should feel ill at ease. Jim was her boyfriend and, even if they were not engaged, it was natural that, in a moment of exultation, he should kiss her.

"They're ready for us," Madge said, as she replaced the telephone.

They went down to the projection

room and sat in the semi-darkness as a picture of Jim was projected on to the screen. His voice came over well, deep and resonant, but his reactions to various situations — grief, anger, laughter — seemed, to Madge, rather stilted. However, they seemed to satisfy Miles.

"Okay," the latter said, as the short film flickered to an end, "the part's yours, Jim. Madge will give you a copy of the script. Have a look at it over lunch and be ready for rehearsal at half-past two."

"Thanks!" Jim's eyes shone. "I'll try not to let you down."

Miles nodded; then, excusing himself, hurried away.

"Is he always like this — rushing from one thing to another?" Jim asked, as he and Madge left the projection-room.

She shrugged. "It's the only way he can get through his day. He works very hard — too hard, I sometimes think."

They decided to stay in the building

and have lunch in the canteen. As they carried their trays to a table, Jim said: "I had a letter from my mother this morning. I'd given her your address to write to, until I get settled."

"How is she?" Madge asked.

"All right. It's my father who's not very well. Apparently, he's had a bad cold and has had to stay at home for a few days. I thought he looked a bit peaky when I left home."

"How will the business carry on, now you're here, and your father's ill, Jim?" she asked.

He frowned. "Oh, there's a good foreman. Been with us for years. In any case, Dad's only got a cold. He'll be back at work today."

"I hope he gets on all right. Is your mother very worried?"

"Oh, she can cope," he laughed. "Depend on it, she wouldn't let my father go back to the works if he wasn't fit."

But Madge was not so sure. She had met Mr. Lingard several times and he had struck her as a headstrong man who would take his own course, whatever his wife might say. In that way, Jim was very much like him.

"You'd better look at your script," she told Jim, when they had finished their meal. "Miles won't expect you to know your lines accurately at this first rehearsal, but he'll want you to have a good idea of what you're talking about."

"Stay and have coffee with me, Madge."

Firmly, she shook her head, as she got to her feet. "It's the rehearsal in less than an hour," she said. "Meet me up in the office at a quarter past two and we'll go along to the studio together."

"Okay, chief!" he grinned and, when she glanced back from the door, he had the script open before him, elbows on the table, chin resting in his cupped hands.

6

ALTHOUGH Jim's part was a small one, it needed a certain amount of acting ability. As the innocent country boy, determined to have his fling in the big city, he was the comic relief in what was otherwise a serious story.

Madge, sitting beside Miles in the producer's box, looked down into the studio and smiled. Jim looked very odd, in checked cloth cap and baggy flannel trousers.

At that moment, he was being instructed as to the movements he must make when he came within range of the cameras. His face was serious and he nodded to show that he understood as the floor manager, tape measure and chalk in hand, moved from point to point.

"Right! We'll take your scene again,

Jim," Miles said, speaking into the microphone. "Mary, take your place, please!"

The girl, Mary, played the Carruther's French maid, with whom Jim, as the Yorkshire cousin, falls madly in love at first sight. As soon as he is left alone with her, he begs her to elope with him. The scene went quite smoothly until Jim had to go down on his knees before the maid, and beg her to go with him.

"You're infatuated with the girl," Miles snapped into the microphone, "so for heaven's sake show it. Right! let's try it again."

Jim did his best, but plainly Miles Brent was not satisfied. After the scene had been repeated half a dozen times, Miles said: "All right, leave it for today. We'll have another go at it tomorrow morning. Ten o'clock. Don't be late!"

Madge's heart sank. "He'll be better tomorrow," she said, in a low voice. "After all, it's the first time he's tried anything like this."

Miles smiled. "Don't worry, Madge. I'll knock him into shape in the next two days."

The rehearsal went on. Madge wondered if Jim would go home when he had changed. If he was moving into his new digs he would have quite a few things to do.

It was four o'clock before she was free to go back to her office. To her surprise Jim was there, sitting in the room's only armchair.

He jumped up when she came in. "I thought you were never coming!" he cried, a frown on his face.

"The rehearsal's only just finished," she said. "I didn't expect to find you still here."

He went to stand by the window and looked out on the roofs below.

"I was a flop, wasn't I?" he muttered.

She shook her head. "What nonsense! It was natural that you would find the part a bit strange at first. When you've had another rehearsal you'll do it very well, I'm sure."

He still glared out of the window. "I don't see why Brent had to be so sharp with me," he said. "I'm not a child, though he talked to me as if I were."

"Miles talks to everybody like that, Jim," she said patiently. "I've heard him bawl someone out for half an hour or so, then buy them a drink ten minutes later. It's his way of getting results. There's never any ill feeling about it."

"I'm glad to hear it! Personally, I should have thought a little patience might have got better results."

Madge bit her lip. "Really, Jim, don't you think you're being just a bit childish? It is the producer's job to bring out the best in the actors. He's got to hustle them — "

"So you think I'm being childish, do you?" Jim interrupted her, hotly.

"I shouldn't have said that, perhaps. I just wanted you to understand — "

"I think you're being a bit more than just loyal to your boss, Madge. He's always right and I'm always wrong, it seems to me."

She checked a sudden urgent impulse to lose her temper with him. Instead, she smiled and said quietly:

"You're tired, Jim. Go home. I'll try not to be late leaving the office. Perhaps we can go to the cinema this evening."

But he stood over her now, placing his hands on her desk and looking down into her eyes. His own were angry. "Stop treating me like a spoiled child!" he cried. "I think I interpreted that part fairly well. Brent had no right to make me look a fool in front of all those people."

"You're exaggerating, Jim. He treated you just the same as — "

But Jim wasn't listening. He had turned and made for the door. He glanced back before he left the office. "I shan't be free to take you to the cinema tonight," he said. "I'm moving into my new flat. I shall be busy."

"I'd like to help . . ." she began,

but with: "I can manage quite well!" he disappeared, closing the door sharply behind him.

She sighed, as she turned to her typewriter. How touchy Jim was! She supposed that in Hunsworth he had been used to taking the most important parts in amateur productions.

The door opened and she looked up, expecting to see Miles. Then her heart missed a beat, as she recognized the tall, handsome man who entered the room. It was Terry Black, the most famous all-round entertainer in the country — the man who had directed her when she had lost herself in the scenery storage room. She did not expect him to remember her.

"Hello, there!" he cried, and the famous flashing smile revealed very white teeth.

"Did you want Mr. Brent?" Madge asked.

He nodded. "That's the reason for my visit. Will he be long?" Madge shook her head, and he went on: "I'll sit here and wait for him, if you don't mind."

He sat down in the armchair and smiled at her. "We've met before, haven't we? Oh, yes, I remember! I found you wandering among the scenery, looking utterly lost, and ready to burst into tears."

She was flattered that he remembered so well. He must meet dozens of people every day — far more interesting and exciting than herself.

"It was kind of you to help me when I was lost," she said, smiling shyly. She was a little in awe of this famous personality.

He produced a thin, gold case and offered Madge a cigarette. When she shook her head, he smiled wryly.

"Wise girl! Smoking's a bad habit. If I had any sense, I'd give it up."

She wondered what to say to him. She wondered if he would think her rude if she got on with her work. As she made a tentative move to put some notepaper into her machine, he said: "Are you a Londoner, Miss — Miss . . ."

"Madge Fairley." She shook her head. "No, I come from the North. Hunsworth."

He ran long fingers through his thick hair. "You'll know Casterley fairly well, I suppose?"

Her eyes lit up. Casterley. Why, it was only five miles or so from her home town.

"Yes, I know it well. I have an aunt living there whom I used to visit quite often."

He looked round with exaggerated caution; then, finger to lips, he whispered hoarsely: "Don't breathe the news to a soul, Madge, but I was born in Casterley!"

She eyed him in surprise. She, like countless thousands of his admirers, imagined he was a Londoner. That was the impression he always fostered whenever he appeared on TV. In fact, in variety shows he was often introduced, in respect of his great reputation, as "The Londoner of all Londoners."

She looked at him with a doubtful frown. "You've certainly fooled everybody," she said accusingly.

He winked at her. "Keep it to yourself, darling, but it's the absolute truth!" Still conspiratorial, he glanced over his shoulder at the door, as if afraid someone might overhear him. "I was born in Casterley, twenty-seven years ago. My father was a conjurer, and he was appearing at the local theatre. My mother was standing in the wings, watching him. My father always said it gave him confidence to have her there. Then, suddenly, I began to make my presence felt and my mother was rushed to hospital."

"But you didn't live in Casterley?"

"Only for ten days, until my mother was fit enough to leave. We never stayed in one place for long."

He sat back and eyed her with a pleased air, as if proud and delighted to have impressed her.

"It's most romantic!" she said, suppressing a desire to giggle.

"So I'm really a Yorkshireman," he said, with such an air of gloom that she burst out laughing.

"Is that such an awful thing?"

"It can't be, can it, if you're a Yorkshire lass!" he cried, his whole face lighting up and his eyes twinkling.

He told her other stories about his early life, and though these for the most part kept her almost helpless with laughter, at times she felt a real pity for the little waif who had travelled with his parents from small town to small town, through the length and breadth of the country. He appeared to have been a very pathetic child, starved of security and the companionship of other children.

"I got my chance in Newcastle," he said. "I was ten at the time and my father, who suffered from bronchitis, collapsed in the wings as he was about to go on. My mother didn't know what to do. If my father's act was cancelled there'd be no money."

He laid a long finger along his nose and winked at Madge. "I'd been practising a few songs in our lodgings when my mother and father were out. I was rather proud of myself and I suggested to my mother that I went on, in place of my father. At first she wouldn't agree but, as the curtain went up, I stepped past my father and walked out in front of the floodlights. It was a great moment!"

"You must have been terrified!" Madge whispered.

"No, I wasn't. I was rather amused, as a matter of fact, for naturally the orchestra leader didn't know I was coming and hadn't a clue what music to play. So I sang one of my songs without any accompaniment whatever. It was a huge success!"

"What happened after that?"

"Oh, the manager came on and apologized that my father hadn't appeared as announced. But the audience demanded another song from me and there was nothing the manager could do about it. The orchestra leader found out what songs I proposed to sing and gave me all the backing I required. After that, I kept my mother and father until Dad died, a year later. My mother — God bless her — is still full of beans and lives here, in London."

Madge could have gone on listening indefinitely, but just then the door opened and Miles hurried into the room. He nodded to Terry Black. "Hello, Terry, what brings you slumming to the drama department?" he grinned.

"I'm giving a party tonight," Terry replied. "I want you and Pat to come along — that is, if you're free."

"I don't think we're doing anything else. I'll ring her and find out, if you like." He glanced at Madge. "I think she should be at her flat, Madge. Get her on the phone, will you, please?"

A few seconds later, Madge heard his fiancée's oversweet voice at the other end of the line.

"Mr. Brent would like a word with

you, Miss Carnford," Madge said, and handed the receiver to Miles.

Terry came a little closer to her desk. "How about your coming, too?" he asked her. "I think you'd find it quite fun. There are quite a number of famous celebrities coming along."

It was on the tip of her tongue to refuse. Then she remembered how Jim had told her he could manage to move into his new digs quite well without her help. She smiled.

"Thank you, Mr. Black," she said. "I'd love to come."

"Why not call me Terry?" he asked. "Mr. Black is very distant and prim."

Miles, replacing the receiver, said that Pat was delighted to accept the invitation. "I'm to pick her up at eight o'clock," he said. "Is that all right?"

"Fine. I've just asked your delightful secretary to come along, too. She says she will."

Madge glanced at Miles. Suppose he objected to her going to the party. After all, he was her boss, and some bosses

99

hated their secretaries encroaching upon their private lives.

But he smiled back at her. "Good for her!" he said, and added: "Will you be able to get there all right?"

"I'll take a taxi."

"Right, I'll give you the address," Terry said, scribbling on a scrap of paper. "I wish I could fetch you in my car; but I'll have to be on the spot. Perhaps I can take you home, when it's over?"

"I'll manage quite well," she said. "It's very kind of you to ask me at all."

"Well, I'll be pushing off," Terry said and, with his gay, twinkling smile much in evidence, he waved his hand and made for the door.

"Has he asked you to bring Jim along with you?" Miles asked, as he went to sit at his own desk.

She shook her head. "He doesn't know I have a boyfriend," she said, and there was something in her tone which made Miles turn to look at her.

"Well, didn't you tell him you were engaged?" he asked in surprise.

She frowned. "But I'm not engaged! Oh, Jim and I are good friends, but . . . "

"I thought there was some sort of understanding — ?"

"I suppose there is, but-well, it's not the same as being officially engaged."

He eyed her thoughtfully for a few seconds. "You haven't quarrelled with Jim, have you?"

"Why should you think that?" She was conscious of the colour rising to her cheeks.

"I don't know. Just an impression I got. Forget it!"

He turned to the papers on his desk, then told her to get her notebook ready. For the next hour, he dictated; then, with a glance at his watch, he said they'd both better leave if they were to go home and change before Terry Black's party.

. . . To Madge's relief, Jim was not in the flat when she let herself in. Jenny came out of the small kitchen.

"How about an omelet?" she asked.

"I'm going to a party," Madge announced. "I don't really feel like much to eat."

"A party! How exciting. Who's giving it? Miles Brent?"

"No, Terry Black."

Jenny's mouth fell open. "You're joking! Not the Terry Black?"

"The one and only! He came into the office this afternoon, to invite Miles, and he asked me as well."

"Good for you! What will you wear?"

"I rather hoped you'd lend me your black skirt and pink top."

"You're welcome. You can have my mother's stole as well, if you like."

"You're an angel!" Madge cried. "By the way, have you seen Jim?"

"He went off to his new flat, taking his suitcase with him. I suppose he feels, as he's paid a week in advance, he might as well take advantage of it."

"I offered to help him move in, but he was quite happy to do it on his own," Madge said, her smile fading.

"Yes, he seemed a bit sulky. You two haven't fallen out, have you?"

"We had a few words, nothing more. And now I must dash. I want a bath, and you know what that geyser's like!"

As Madge lay in the warm water, ten minutes later, her emotions were mixed. One part of her wanted to get dressed and hurry off to the new flat and make it up with Jim, the other urged her to teach Jim a lesson, to let him see that she was not always available — at the mercy of his every mood and whim.

As she dressed, she tried to put Jim out of her mind. She had promised Terry Black she would go to his party, and both he and Miles would think it odd if she didn't turn up.

She pirouetted before the mirror in her borrowed finery. Jenny's separates — a black silk skirt and shell-pink top — might have been bought for her. When she added the fur stole she hardly recognized herself.

"Oh, very elegant indeed!" Jenny said, coming into the room.

"Thanks to you," Madge laughed, her eyes dancing, her red lips parted in excitement.

"A pity Jim can't see you now," Jenny declared. "I doubt if he'd have gone off to that dreary little room of his, if he'd known what he was missing."

Madge's smile faded. "I'd better hurry. I'll have to take a taxi."

"I should certainly think so. You can't go on a bus, looking like that. I'll ring the taxi rank."

Five minutes later, Madge was being driven, tense and excited, towards the West End.

Terry Black's flat was in Mayfair, in a fashionable street not far from the bright lights of Piccadilly.

When she had paid the taxi fare, outside the big block of flats, Madge rather hesitantly entered the imposing entrance hall, with its deep pile carpet that made her feel that she was walking on air. A blue uniformed doorman greeted her.

"May I help you, madam?" he asked.

"I want Mr. Black's flat," she replied.

"Number sixteen on the sixth floor, madam," the doorman said, and led her to the lift and gave instructions to the lift-boy. The lift moved smoothly up to the sixth floor.

A thick carpet muffled the sound of Madge's footsteps as she walked along the softly lit corridor. Outside number sixteen, she paused. There was still time to turn and go back to the lift. If she took a taxi, she could be safely home with Jenny again in less than twenty minutes.

Something warned her not to go through the door facing her. Something told her that she was not going to enjoy the party. She hesitated . . .

Then the lift doors opened again and a gay party of young men and girls emerged, laughing and talking.

As they headed towards her, she guessed that they, too, must be going to Terry Black's party.

They stared at her curiously as they approached, obviously wondering why she did not ring the bell. Raising her hand, she put her finger on the white button, and pressed it.

7

"**D**ARLINGS!**"

Terry Black, startlingly handsome in dinner suit and black bow-tie, arms wide in welcome, stood in the doorway. The famous smile lit up his clean-cut features.

The little party behind Madge swept her forward and she found herself in a big entrance hall. She was ushered into the small cloakroom adjoining the hall, and left her fur wrap there.

A hubbub of sound came from an inner room. Terry led Madge and the people who had arrived with her into a big lounge, with furniture pushed against the walls to accommodate the throng of people filling the room.

"Have a drink!"

A waiter, carrying a tray, was passing at that moment and Terry seized a glass and handed it to Madge.

"I'm glad you came, Madge!" he said.

"It was nice of you to ask me," she murmured rather awkwardly, sipping the drink, which she did not particularly like.

"Forgive me if I leave you now," he said. "I must go and greet some guests. Make yourself at home."

She stood, a little self-consciously, alone in the middle of the room. She wondered if Miles and Pat Carnford had arrived yet.

A tall young man, with horn-rimmed spectacles and an earnest look on his sallow face, came to her side.

"Are you on television?" he asked, looking at her over the rim of the glass he was holding.

She shook her head. "No, I'm secretary to a producer," she replied.

"To a producer, eh?"

"Yes, to Miles Brent."

He regarded her with increasing interest. "I'm Mervyn Taylor. I've been in one or two things with Metropolitan

TV. Do you happen to know if there are any likely parts going in Brent's new production?"

She had been approached before by aspiring actors, and had a stock reply. "I really couldn't tell you," she said. "The casting department handles that sort of thing. Mr. Brent has little say in the matter of engaging actors."

He lost interest in her instantly and wandered away. Before anyone could take his place, Terry returned and took her arm.

"Come into the other room," he said. He opened an inner door and Madge saw a dozen or so people grouped about a table. On this was set a roulette wheel. As Terry and Madge entered, the croupier — a swarthy individual in a white dinner jacket and red bow-tie — invited the players to make their bets.

"Like to try?" Terry asked.

"I don't think so, thanks," Madge said. "Perhaps I could just watch for a few minutes."

He shrugged. "Just as you like. It is quite interesting." Before he left her, he said: "Forgive me if I leave you. I must circulate, or my other guests will have something to say. But you will let me run you home after the party, won't you? I can't have you going out into the London streets on your own to look for a taxi."

"It's very kind of you," she said. "But I don't want to put you to a lot of trouble."

"It won't be any trouble. I'll be glad to do it!"

When he had gone, she stood watching the players. There were three women in the group about the table. Madge recognized a well-known stage star and several others whose faces were vaguely familiar. They seemed to be taking the gambling very seriously.

"Why don't you have a flutter, darling?" one of the women asked, looking over her shoulder at Madge.

"I've just made fifteen pounds."

"Thanks, I prefer to watch," Madge replied.

She began to feel uncomfortable. Perhaps these people didn't welcome her silent presence. Perhaps they found her distracting. Even the croupier had glanced with a frown in her direction more than once.

The door opened and someone came into the room. Madge, glancing round, saw Miles smiling at her.

"So this is where you are?" he said. "I wondered if, after all, you had decided not to come."

Her heart lightened on seeing him. He glanced at the table.

"I hope you haven't been losing your hard-earned money," he said with a laugh, but there was a serious note underlying the lightness of his tone. "Terry's parties can get a bit hectic at times, especially when it comes to gambling."

"You can put your mind at rest," she smiled. "I can't afford to take part,

111

even if I wanted to — which I don't."

They went back to the other room. Madge saw that Patricia Carnford was surrounded by a circle of admirers. It looked to Madge as if she had abandoned Miles as soon as she had arrived at the party.

Or had Miles possibly abandoned her, to seek his secretary?

As this thought came to Madge, the colour came into her cheeks. Why on earth should Miles Brent leave his attractive fiancée to search for his secretary, the minute he arrived at the party? He must have discovered her by pure chance.

The noise in the big lounge seemed more overpowering than before, and Miles frowned.

"You can hardly hear yourself speak!" he declared. "I don't know why I bother to come to these sort of affairs. Still, Pat enjoys them — "

Terry came up. He put one arm round Miles's shoulders, the other about Madge's.

"I'm glad you two have got together," he said. "Have another drink. I'll be able to give you a little more time very soon, Madge. The guests have all arrived."

"How do you like Terry?" Miles asked, as the other excused himself and hurried over to a beautiful blonde girl who was beckoning to him.

"He seems very good-natured and kind," Madge replied.

Miles was silent for a few seconds, then he said seriously: "Be careful, Madge. Terry's a popular chap, but he's always had things too easy. His reputation with women isn't too good."

Madge felt angry. Miles was talking to her as though she were a very young, innocent girl — as though she needed to be warned against worldly men like Terry Black. Well, she was old enough and wise enough to decide for herself who should be her friends.

"He told me a little about his childhood," she said, a certain constraint showing in her manner. "He certainly didn't seem to find things too easy then."

"You should feel flattered," he smiled. "He doesn't often talk about his younger days. Where was he brought up — in an orphanage?"

"Not as bad as that," she said sharply, "but he had a pretty unstable childhood."

At that moment, an elderly man with a distinguished face and silver hair came up and introduced himself to Miles. Madge was relieved to see Terry approaching and greeted him with a smile. He took her arm. "Like to see round my flat?" he asked.

She was delighted to. The tour included a glance into the big, American-style kitchen, with its battery of labour-saving devices and startlingly white walls under white strip lighting. Then to the big bedroom, with its expensive light walnut furniture, its enormous bed with quilted headboard, its scarlet carpet and velvet curtains. The bathroom was a dream with a sunken marble bath and mirrored walls . . .

"It's lovely, Terry," Madge sighed. "Like something out of a film."

"You must come again — when there aren't so many people here," he murmured, and something in his eyes and the tone of his voice made her look quickly away.

After that, the evening passed swiftly. Terry introduced Madge to several people, most of whom she had seen about the studios or on the stage and films. She tried not to feel inadequate as she listened to their witty, sophisticated conversation, but she found it impossible to be completely at ease.

Presently, a lavish buffet supper was served. Madge found herself standing next to Miles and, although he was keeping up a steady conversation with a glamorous, middle-aged actress, he turned now and then to smile at Madge. As Madge returned his smile, she glanced behind his shoulder and saw Pat staring angrily at them. Pure jealousy showed in her eyes, making them glittery and hard. At that moment, she was almost frightening.

At last, someone suggested that they all go on to a night club, and the guests began to drift out to the cloakroom to collect their things. Madge did not want to go with them, so she hung back in the lounge, not knowing quite what to do. Miles and Pat also remained behind, and stood arguing in one corner of the room. Obviously, Miles did not want to go to the night club, and finally Patricia had to sulkily agree to be driven straight home.

As the room emptied, Madge began to wonder whether Terry had changed his mind about running her home. Surely he would want to go with his other guests to the night club.

She went out into the hall to find him.

"Terry, I can easily get a taxi," she said.

He shook his head. "Nonsense! I

shan't be more than a few minutes. Wait in the lounge!"

So he was not accompanying his other guests after all.

It was a full half-hour before the front door closed behind the last guest, and he came to sit beside her on the couch.

"Now, let's have a little drink together before I run you home," he said, but she shook her head.

She had already put on Jenny's wrap and was ready to go. "It's late, Terry," she said. "I really should be going home. I start at the office at nine-thirty, you know."

He slipped his arm about her slim waist. "Don't be a spoil-sport, darling," he murmured, and his lips brushed her hair.

She pulled quickly away. "I'll get a taxi," she said, standing up and making for the door. "It will save your having to turn out."

But he went after her, grabbing her arm. A shadow had passed over his face. Gone was the bright smile, the charming manner.

"What's the matter with you?" he demanded. "You surely didn't expect I'd let you go straight home, did you? A pretty girl like you must sing for her supper."

Then she recalled what Miles had said, earlier in the evening — something she had felt was unfair. "His reputation with women isn't too good," Miles had said and she had chosen to ignore the warning.

She pulled desperately away from Terry. But, as she made another attempt to reach the door, his hand reached out and grabbed her shoulder. He swung her round and the next moment she was in his arms, his lips — fierce, demanding — on hers.

"Let me go! Let me go!" she gasped, struggling to be free.

But he did not heed her struggles, only held her more tightly, his mouth seeking hers.

Suddenly, she drew back her right

foot, and kicked him sharply on the shin. The pointed toe of her shoe did its work, and Terry jumped back with a cry of pain. Now was the opportunity to escape!

She reached the hall, but he came hobbling after her, almost beside himself with fury.

"I'll teach you to kick me, you vicious little wretch!" he cried.

Desperately, she seized the latch and turned it. The door came half-open.

Terry's hands gripped her arms again but, even as she drew breath to scream, a familiar voice broke in: "Is anything wrong, Madge?"

Miles Brent pushed the door wide and came into the hall. Seeing him, Terry Black stepped back from Madge.

"Miles! What are you doing here?" he asked, nervously fumbling with his bow-tie.

The other did not reply. Looking at the frightened girl, he said quietly: "Are you ready to go, Madge?"

She nodded. She dare not trust

herself to speak. Without even glancing at Terry Black, she went past Miles and out into the corridor.

Miles followed her and closed the door of the flat behind him. He said nothing on the way to the lift, and it was Madge who spoke first, as they made their way down to the ground floor.

"But, Miles, I — I thought you went home ages ago," she said, her voice quivering dangerously.

"I took Pat home, then decided to come back to see if you had left," he said simply. "You see, I know what Terry's like. I did try to warn you, but obviously you didn't believe me and had to find out for yourself."

Suddenly, Madge felt the tears well up in her eyes and run down her cheeks. She groped for her bag but, before she could get it open, Miles had thrust his own handkerchief into her hand.

There was no one in the entrance hall as they passed through. Miles's car was just outside and he helped her into it, gently. He was being very kind.

He said little on the way home. Once she glanced at him, but his stern profile told her little.

Thank goodness he had come back. It suddenly occurred to her that she had not yet thanked him.

"Miles, I'm very grateful to you for — for coming back like that," she whispered.

For a moment he looked at her. A faint smile came to his lips. "Thank goodness I did," he said, and added: "But, somehow, I think you're more capable of looking after yourself than I imagined. Terry's used to the girl doing all the chasing. He doesn't usually have to put up much of a fight."

Remembering the painful kick she had administered to Terry's shin, Madge smiled to herself. Maybe, if Miles hadn't turned up when he did, Terry might, at that moment, have been begging her for mercy!

Madge was already feeling more

composed and, when Miles drew the car up outside the flat, the feeling of displeasure which had assailed her after the episode in Terry Black's flat, had almost left her.

"See you in the morning, Madge," Miles said.

She nodded. "And thanks once again, Miles," she murmured, and opened the door on her side.

The catch was an unfamiliar one, and he went round the car to help her out. Neither of them saw the dark figure in the shadows at the foot of the steps leading up to the front door of the house.

Jim Lingard had seen the car come into the street as he left the house. He had been waiting with Jenny hoping to see Madge when she got home from the party. But when she had not turned up, he had decided to go back to his own digs. Hearing the car, he had slipped into the shadows, to see who was driving Madge home.

Miles held Madge's arm as he walked

with her to the foot of the steps.

"Sleep well!" he smiled, and waited until she had climbed the steps to the front door, had inserted her key in the lock and, with a last wave, had disappeared into the dark hall.

Jim hesitated. Should he step out and tell Miles Brent that he resented his spending so much time with the girl he was to marry?

Then he remembered that, within the next few days, he would be appearing in *The Carruther's Family* — a Miles Brent production. His success in that meant a great deal to him. It would be silly to antagonize Miles just before it took place.

So he stayed where he was, his eyes bitter, watching Miles get back into the car, and drive away.

When the car had gone Jim stood in the street, looking up at the window of the flat above. Should he go up now and challenge Madge, demand to know if there was something between herself and Miles?

No, better to sleep on it. There was plenty of time. He hurried away and walked down the street — a miserable, jealous, and very tired young man.

* * *

Jenny looked round her bedroom door as Madge went into the flat. "Did you see Jim?" she asked. "He left only a few minutes ago."

Madge shook her head. "I must have just missed him. There was no sign of him when I came into the house."

"Did someone bring you home?" Jenny asked curiously.

"Yes, Miles Brent." It was on the tip of Madge's tongue to tell her friend the whole story, then she decided against it. She was tired out, and all she wanted to do was to go to bed.

"What did Jim want?" she asked, as she handed Jenny her stole.

"Why, to see you, of course!" the other laughed. "He seemed quite put out when I told him that you were at a party. He decided to wait — then, when it struck midnight, he said he'd go back to his digs. I suppose he thought I was tired and wanting to get to bed."

"He knows very well I wouldn't have gone to the party if he had wanted me to help him move into the new flat," Madge said, then turned away. "I really must get to bed. There's stacks of work piling up at the office and I mustn't be late."

Jenny watched her walk along to her room. When the bedroom door had closed behind Madge, Jenny's face became suddenly very solemn. With a sigh, she went into her bedroom. If only Jim Lingard had never come to the flat to awaken these longings in her lonely heart . . .

Madge, in spite of an unsettled night, was early at the office. Miles came in, a few minutes later, and they were able to clear certain routine work that had to be completed before they went along to the studio, for the final rehearsal and pre-recording of the episode of *The Carruthers Family* in which Jim was to appear. Madge was glad that 'The Carruthers' was pre-recorded. At least, any mistakes Jim made could be corrected before the public saw the episode.

Notebook and pencil in hand, Madge stood a little behind Miles as he addressed the cast. He had certain last-minute instructions to give them, including his critical comments on the last rehearsal.

Madge saw Jim standing behind the little group of actors and actresses. He seemed to be avoiding her gaze, though she tried to catch his eye, so that she could give him a smile of encouragement.

When she did not succeed, she went across to him while Miles was talking to the two principal characters.

"Good luck, Jim!" she said — and, when he did not speak: "I'm sorry I missed you last night!"

For the first time he met her eyes.

"Are you?" he muttered, but before she could say any more Miles's voice reached her.

"All right, take your places everyone! Madge, I'm going up to the box now."

She glanced at Jim again but already he had turned away. There was nothing for it but to follow Miles to the producer's box, overlooking the sitting-room set, in which the first scene was to be played.

The morning passed without incident. The rehearsal was going well.

"Okay. Go and get some lunch and be back here at half-past one," Miles said into the microphone.

Madge looked for Jim but he was not in sight. He had appeared in an earlier scene and had probably already gone to lunch.

"Better go and get something to eat," Miles said. "I'm having some sandwiches here. I've still some last details to settle with the cameramen and the floor director."

"Are you sure you won't want me?"

"No! I'll see you back here with the others at half-past one."

He turned and hurried off. Madge made for the canteen. If she saw Jim there she would explain that she had only gone to Terry Black's party because he had turned down her offer to help him settle into the flat.

But there was no sign of Jim in the canteen. Evidently, he was keeping out of her way. She felt suddenly angry. Why was he behaving like a spoilt child?

As she collected a tray she decided that, as soon as possible, she would have it out with Jim. If he had any grievance against her, she would at least find out what it was.

At half-past one everyone was in position.

"Okay, let's go!" Miles said into the microphone, and Madge settled back to watch Jim. She held her breath as he appeared, and began to speak. A thrill ran through her. This was no longer a rehearsal, but the real thing.

However, she was disappointed. Jim's performance was stiff and unnatural, but Miles did not ask for the scene to be repeated. Perhaps she was over-critical. It was often the way, when watching the performance of someone as close as Jim was to her. Only perfection was good enough . . .

The afternoon wore on and, although the play, when shown to the television audience, would only last half an hour, Miles asked for so many retakes that it was six o'clock before the pre-recording was completed.

"Right, that's it, then," Miles said. "Thank you all!"

He followed Madge from the producer's box and they went upstairs together to the office.

"Not bad, not bad at all," Miles said. "Mary is a pretty smart kid, Madge. She could be really good one day."

Madge waited for him to say something about Jim — but he didn't. He opened the office door and she went into the room ahead of him.

Jim was sitting in the chair beside Miles's desk. He got to his feet as the producer followed Madge into the room.

"Hello, Jim, I thought you'd gone home," Miles smiled.

"I've been waiting here for over an hour," Jim replied.

He did not return Miles's smile nor did he look at Madge.

"I suppose you've been waiting for Madge," Miles said. "I'm sorry I've kept her so long."

"I came to see you!" Jim said, and there was a note of strain in his voice. "I wanted to have your candid opinion of my performance this afternoon."

Miles frowned. "Oh, can't it wait, Jim? I'm tired, and I've still quite a lot to do before I can go home."

"No, it can't wait!" He stood before Miles's desk and his eyes glittered. "I want to know now."

Miles sat back in his chair and shrugged. "Very well, if that's how you feel," he said quietly. "I'm afraid your performance didn't quite come up to my expectations, Jim. That could be because you've not settled into the TV medium yet. It's very different from appearing in amateur stage productions with your friends. After all, it doesn't matter if you make the grade or not in those circumstances; but here — when you're acting with professionals — it rather shows up when . . . "

"When one's an amateur, eh?" Jim's voice was bitter.

"Well, yes, if you like to put it like that," Miles said. "But don't take what I say too much to heart, old man. We all have to learn, you know."

"Which means you won't be too eager to give me another part, is that it?" Jim demanded.

"I might be able to give you something else a little later. Just now, there's nothing suitable coming up — "

"Why won't you be honest and admit that you don't intend to give me another opportunity?" Jim said bitterly.

Miles shrugged. "Because that isn't necessarily true. Just now, I think you need to study other people's work. Watch some of the real professionals for a while. Then come back to me — "

Jim's eyes narrowed. "Thank you very much! But I don't see myself hanging round your office, Mr. Brent, on the off-chance of your giving me another part in the dim and distant future." He looked at Madge. "Are you ready?"

Madge glanced at Miles who had turned rather wearily away. He had had a hard day and didn't really feel up to arguing with Jim any more.

"You can go, Madge," he said. "I shan't want you again tonight." Abruptly, he swung on his heel and hurried from the office.

Madge felt her anger rising as she looked at Jim. Never before had she seen him in this sort of mood and at this moment she felt she hated him!

"I don't know how you could talk to Miles in that way — after all his kindness!" she cried.

Jim looked at her with raised eyebrows. "You don't? I suppose it hasn't occurred to you that he's found fault with everything I've done at rehearsals!"

"But that's not true, Jim. In my opinion, he's been very patient with you."

"You really are taking his side now, aren't you?"

"I'm only being fair. Miles has done his utmost to coax the best out of you. You — you just didn't respond, that's all."

"That's rich, I must say! Why, if I'd been left alone, I wouldn't have been so nervous. As it was, I just couldn't relax with Brent constantly criticising me. Once or twice, I hardly knew whether I was coming or going!"

She looked at him in despair. How could Jim be like this? She could understand his being upset and disappointed that he had not done better, but to blame it all on to Miles was too unfair for words.

"I think you'd better go home and get a good night's sleep, Jim," she said coldly. "In the morning, I'm sure you'll see things in a better light."

He looked at her with sudden suspicion. "I suppose you're waiting for Brent to take you home!"

"Why should I?" she demanded. "You heard him say I could go. He expected me to go with you."

"He wanted me to think that, but I've no doubt he expects to find you still here when he comes back!"

She lost her temper then. "Oh, Jim, you are absurd! Why should he expect to find me still here, when he's told me to go?"

He hesitated, then burst out: "Because he know's you're head over heels in love with him." And before she could speak: "Oh, I saw you saying good night to him last night after the party. It seems to me, there's far more between you and Brent than there should be between a man and his secretary!"

Tears rushed into her eyes. She tried to say something but the words would not come.

As for Jim, he rushed to the door, threw it open and disappeared.

Madge sank back in her chair. Of all the fantastic things to happen! She had never realized that Jim could be so furiously jealous.

She dried her eyes, then decided she'd better go along to the cloakroom to repair her make up. It would never do for Miles — or anybody else, for that matter — to come in and find her with a tear-streaked face.

As Jim rushed from the building he almost collided with Patricia Carnford, who had parked her car, a few seconds before, and was on her way to meet Miles.

"Why, hello!" she exclaimed. "You're certainly in a great hurry!" She fluttered long lashes at Jim as she regarded him from blue eyes.

If Jim had not been in such a highly emotional state he might have held back the words that rushed to his lips. "I'm glad I've seen you, Miss Carnford," he cried. "I think it's time you had a few words with that fiancé of yours."

"I beg your pardon!" She was startled. What on earth did this man mean by shouting at her like this? Previously he had been rather nice to her, and she had been prepared to be gracious to him; but she could not allow him to bawl at her like that.

"How dare you shout at me!" She almost choked with anger as he stood before her, obviously wondering what to say next.

He bit his lip. "You are still engaged to Miles Brent, aren't you?" he demanded.

"Yes, I am! Is there any reason why I shouldn't be?"

"None at all, but I think you should insist he stops poaching on other people's preserves!"

"Meaning?"

"That, at the moment, he's showing

far too much interest in my girlfriend. As you're engaged to him, it's up to you to see he behaves himself!"

Then he was gone, his long legs carrying him swiftly across the car park in the direction of the main gate.

Oblivious of the curious eyes of people passing in and out of the building, Patricia stood there for nearly two minutes.

Ordinarily, if anyone had told her that Miles was interested in his secretary, she would have laughed such a story to scorn. But Jim Lingard's anger had been genuine. Evidently, he had just left Miles and Madge, perhaps having caught them kissing in the office.

She remembered how, on the previous night, Miles had almost gone out of his way to be with his secretary at Terry Black's party. Suppose — suppose he was falling in love with the girl!

But he can't, Patricia thought in despair. He's engaged to me.

Suddenly she realised how important was her forthcoming marriage. Just

137

lately, she had not been in so much demand as in the past. Producers were not quite as eager to offer her parts. Just lately, she had found it necessary to watch her diet, and her beautician had become far more important to her. She was still beautiful, but she was thirty, and the first bloom of youth had gone.

In her scheme of things, Miles represented a secure future. Even if her career as an actress was not yet over, she did not mean to be left in the position, in later years, of having to beg for parts. She intended to retire gracefully, to be the wife of a successful man, who was wealthy enough to provide her with all the good things of life.

Her eyes narrowed as she turned to go into the building.

So that girl is getting ideas about Miles, is she? she thought as, ignoring the commissionaire's salute, she made for the lift. "It's up to you," that young man had said. Right, I'll cook that little upstart's goose, once and for all! It may not be today or tomorrow, but I'll do it as soon as I've thought something out.

She went along to Miles's office and, after a light knock, opened the door.

The room was empty. Miles had not returned and Madge was still in the cloakroom.

As she looked across at Madge's empty desk an idea leapt into Patricia Carnford's scheming mind.

Glancing down at the expensive bracelet she was wearing — Miles had given it to her when they had become engaged, some months before — she slipped it off her slender wrist.

Crossing to Madge's desk, she opened the centre drawer. The drawer was full of envelopes and headed notepaper. Raising the pile of notepaper, Pat slipped the bracelet underneath, arranged the things on top to hide the slight bulge and then closed the drawer. She went to the door and opened it. The corridor outside was as deserted as when she had arrived, a minute before.

A moment later she was in the lift again, descending to the ground floor.

Only the commissionaire saw her go back to her car. He may have wondered at the brevity of her visit, then forgot all about her as the telephone at his side rang and he reached for the receiver.

That evening, when Miles turned up to take Pat out to dinner, she was in great distress.

"Miles, darling!" she cried, rushing to him and throwing her arms about his neck, "I've got a most awful confession to make."

"Good heavens, Pat, what's the matter?" he demanded. "You sound as if you've robbed the Bank of England."

"It's not quite as bad as that, darling," she murmured, "but I know you'll be angry with me. I — I've lost that lovely, lovely bracelet you gave me when we got engaged."

He laughed. "Well, don't take on so, Pat. See, I'm not a bit angry. I seem to remember that you have lost things before!"

But tears rolled down Pat's cheeks and she would not be comforted by Miles.

"I've searched and searched absolutely everywhere," she wailed. "Oh, darling, I just can't bear to think I'll never see my bracelet again. It means so much to me, just because — you gave it to me."

He kissed her lightly. "If you don't find it, I promise I'll buy you another," he said.

"But I don't want another, darling! I want that very bracelet. Oh, can't you see? Nothing could ever replace it."

"Perhaps you haven't looked far enough yet," he suggested, though he was tired and wanted something to eat.

"It certainly isn't in the flat! I've even looked under the carpets."

"Did you lose it in the street? I seem to remember your telling me the catch was loose."

"I meant to have it repaired. Oh, I don't deserve to have such a lovely bracelet." Her sobs grew louder. "I'll never be happy again, if it doesn't turn up."

"We'll report its loss to the police, tomorrow," Miles said. "I'm sure you'll soon have it back."

"I could have lost it at the studios, I suppose," she mused.

"Maybe you did. I'll mention it, in the morning."

"I've been in and out of your office in the last day or so.

"But if it was there, either Madge or I would have seen it."

She nodded. "Yes, of course you would, darling. I hadn't thought of that. Will you promise to have a search made throughout the building. I shan't be happy unless you say you will."

To placate her, he nodded. "I promise. And now let's go and get something to eat. I'm famished."

There was a little smile on Pat's face as she went into the bedroom for her coat. So far, so good. The first part of her plan had gone without a hitch.

8

IN the morning, when they had been working for a while, Miles suddenly looked up from his desk and across at Madge.

"By the way, Madge, Pat's lost her bracelet," he said. "She's asked me to mention it, in case you've heard of it being found in the building."

Madge shook her head.

"I'm very sorry! But I'm afraid nobody's said any thing to me. I do hope it turns up soon."

"I'm afraid she only has herself to blame," he said ruefully. "She knew the catch was loose, but didn't take it to a jeweller to be repaired."

"I'll mention it to the other girls when I talk to them at lunch-time," Madge promised.

But no one had heard of a bracelet being found, and Madge reported this to Miles when she returned from lunch.

He smiled. "I shouldn't worry any more about it. I know that Pat's rather careless about such things. She's probably found it somewhere in her flat. It would never occur to her to ring me and let me know the search could be called off."

That afternoon, when Miles was out of the office, Pat came in.

"I'm afraid Miles isn't here," Madge said.

Pat did not say anything for a moment. Madge, seeing her frown, wondered if she objected to her fiancé's secretary calling him by his first name. Yet, Miles had told her he preferred it.

"Will he be back soon?" Pat wanted to know.

"I can't really say," Madge replied. "He's with Mr. Manson, the script-writer. Would you like to wait?"

"Er, no, thank you! I'll come back later," Pat said, and turned to go.

"Did you find your bracelet?" Madge

called after her. "Miles told me it was missing."

Pat gave her an odd look, and for some reason Madge felt uneasy. Why was Pat looking at her like that? It was as if the other girl wanted to say something to her but did not quite know how to do so.

"No, it hasn't turned up yet," Pat muttered; then, without another glance, hurried from the office.

Madge soon forgot her. She had too much work to finish before she went home that night, to waste time speculating about Miles's temperamental fiancée.

About twenty minutes later, Pat saw Miles come out of Tim Manson's office. She had been waiting for him and now she darted forward.

"Why, Pat, what are you doing here?" Miles cried; then, before she could speak, he added quickly, "I'm not ready to go yet. I've still got some work to finish before I leave."

"I want to talk to you, Miles," Pat

said. "It's very urgent."

"But what's it about, dear?" he asked, with a frown. He was impatient to get down on paper some of the ideas he and Tim Manson had just been discussing.

"Can't we go and have a cup of tea somewhere?" she persisted. "I want to talk to you about my bracelet."

"Has it turned up? I thought you'd find it if you looked long enough."

She shook her head. "No, it hasn't turned up. But — something else has."

He noted the strain in her voice and looked a little more closely at her. Her lovely face was distressed and there were tears in her eyes.

"What is it, Pat?" he asked; then, taking her arm, he drew her along the corridor. "We'll go into the canteen and get you a cup of tea. It should be quiet just now."

As they walked along, he saw, out of the corner of his eye, that her lips were trembling. He heard her give a stifled sob and his bewilderment increased. What on earth had happened to Pat?

He had never known her be so upset.

He told her to sit at a table in the corner of the canteen, and fetched two cups of tea.

"Now, what is it?" he demanded. "You seem quite upset."

"I am upset, Miles," she sobbed, as she wiped the tears from her eyes with a lace handkerchief. "It's a letter I've had."

"A letter? From whom?"

Patricia opened her handbag and took out an envelope.

"That's the whole point," she said in a low voice. "I don't know."

She handed the envelope over. He saw that the name and address were typed. The postmark was a London one.

Frowning, he took the single sheet of notepaper out and unfolded it.

When he had read it, his eyes were shocked. He stared at Pat in sheer disbelief.

"But this is ridiculous! This letter accuses Madge of stealing your bracelet!"

"Yes, I know. That's why I brought it straight to you. I couldn't believe it, when I first opened it."

"And I hope you don't believe it now," he cried.

He examined the letter carefully. It was typed on cheap notepaper and merely signed 'A well-wisher.' Its contents were brief and to the point. The author accused Madge of finding the bracelet outside Miles's office and of not handing it in to the Lost Property Office.

Miles looked at Pat. "But this is all nonsense! I know Madge. If she found your bracelet she would return it instantly. This letter's obviously been written by someone who wants to make trouble. I wonder who can have written it. Who knows about the bracelet being lost, Pat?"

She wrinkled her forehead as she thought about it.

"I've told lots of people," she said. "I mentioned it, so that if anyone heard anything about a bracelet being found they could contact me."

"So plenty of people in this building would know it was missing?"

"Yes! It's possible that one of them might have seen your secretary pick up the bracelet — "

Miles stared at her for a minute before he spoke. Then, in a low voice, he asked: "Are you trying to tell me that you believe Madge is a thief, Pat?"

She shrugged. "What else can I think? After all, what do you know of her, Miles? She hasn't worked for you long. What was she before that?"

"She came from the typing pool, where she had a reputation for being hardworking and trustworthy."

"And before that?"

"She came to London from the north. She — "

She laid her hand over his. "I'm terribly sorry, Miles. This must have come as a big shock to you. I . . . "

Miles stood up. His face was pale; his mouth was set in a thin, hard line.

"We're going along to my office at once, Pat," he said. "I'm going to show this letter to Madge. I think at least we owe that to her. And if she tells me she thinks it is just some spiteful person trying to stir up trouble — as I do — I shall leave it at that."

A flush came into Pat's cheeks.

"And suppose I don't feel like leaving it at that?" she asked. "Perhaps my opinion of your precious Miss Fairley isn't as high as yours, Miles."

Their eyes met and the only sound was the harshness of their breathing. Suddenly, Miles swung on his heel and hurried from the canteen. After a moment Pat followed, and there was a cold glitter in her blue eyes.

In the office, Madge was coping with the morning's correspondence. Coming to the end of her notepaper, she opened the drawer of her desk to get more.

She noticed that there was a slight bump, as if there were something under the notepaper. As she raised the edge of the paper and caught sight of what lay beneath, a horrified little gasp left her lips.

Pat's bracelet! She recognized it instantly.

What on earth was it doing in her desk drawer?

She stretched out her hand and picked it up. Someone must have found it and decided to hide it in her drawer. Perhaps they had meant to return later, when the office was empty, and retrieve it.

As she was holding it, the door opened and Miles and Pat came into the room. The suddenness of their appearance took her aback. She stared at them, seeing the accusing look on the girl's face, the consternation in the man's eyes.

"I — I . . . " she began but could get no farther. For some reason, the words stuck in her throat.

"So the letter-writer was telling the truth," Pat said, unable to keep the note of triumph from her voice.

She had been thinking, as she

followed Miles back to his office, that it might still be difficult to pin the theft of the bracelet on Madge. After all, even if the girl was told about the anonymous letter she might still refuse to let her drawer be searched.

Of course, Pat had intended forcing the issue by demanding that Madge submit to a search. The girl could hardly refuse without appearing guilty. Then the bracelet would be found by Miles or herself — and that would be that!

But now the girl had done the work for her. She looked the very picture of guilt sitting there, the sparkling bracelet in her hand.

"Where did you get the bracelet, Madge?" Miles asked.

"I — I — found it in my drawer," she replied — and, even as she spoke, she knew her story must sound very weak.

"A likely story!" Pat sneered. "You mean you put it there. You're a thief!"

"Be quiet, Pat!" Miles snapped.

Looking directly at Madge, he said: "Pat says she lost the bracelet yesterday. Has it been in your drawer since then?"

"I don't know," Madge said wretchedly. "I — I hadn't seen it until a minute ago, when I noticed that something had got under the notepaper in the drawer. I found the bracelet and — "

"How much time are you going to waste questioning her?" Pat asked, looking at Miles with angry eyes. "Hadn't you better get the police?"

"The police! What on earth are you talking about?" he demanded.

"But she's a thief! You can't let people like that get away with such things. Why, she'll think she can steal anything she pleases if no one does anything about it."

"Don't be a fool, Pat!" Miles said harshly. "You've got your bracelet back, haven't you? To tell the police would only create a scandal. Besides, Madge's story about finding the bracelet in her drawer may be true."

Pat bit her lip and said no more.

Though she longed to make Madge suffer even more, she knew that caution might be the better policy at this stage.

Bringing the police into the matter would mean showing them the anonymous letter she had told Miles she had received that morning. They might get too inquisitive and unearth the typewriter she had borrowed. That would blow the whole thing wide open.

"Oh, all right," she said at last.

Crossing to Madge's desk, she picked up the bracelet and slipped it on to her wrist.

"You can count yourself lucky that I'm not going to bring in the police," she said. "I'll be guided by my fiancé. But I hope you'll have the decency to go away, so that we don't have to see any more of you."

Madge suddenly got to her feet. Her face was ashen. Her hands were shaking. If only she could get away from this awful room, away from Patricia's triumphant gaze, and Miles's shocked and reproachful eyes.

There was only one way to do that. Suddenly, pushing Pat violently to one side, she made for the door.

"Madge, don't go — !" Miles cried, as she hurried past.

But she did not hear him. Blinded by tears, she groped for the handle and pulled the door open.

The next moment she was gone.

★ ★ ★

Jenny, coming back early from the office, heard the telephone ringing as she came upstairs. Hurriedly opening the door of the flat she lifted the receiver.

She gave the number and a woman's voice said: "This is Mrs. Lingard from Hunsworth. Who's that speaking?"

"Hello, Mrs. Lingard," Jenny cried. "This is Jenny Briggs. I share a flat with Madge Fairley."

"Oh, Jenny love, I've rung up several times before, but I supposed you and Madge were both out at work." The warm northern tones came over the distance to Jenny.

"Yes, I've just got in, Mrs. Lingard. Was it Madge you wanted?"

"No, dear, it was Jim, my son. I know he stayed with you and Madge when he first went to London and I wondered if he'd be calling in to see you both later this evening. I had a letter in which he said he'd got a nice room but he didn't give me a telephone number."

"He might call," Jenny said. "Shall I tell him to ring you back?"

"I wish you would. His Dad's got worse and I think Jim should come home to see him."

"I'm sorry to hear such news, Mrs. Lingard. I'll tell you what I'll do. I'll pop round to Jim's flat and see he gets in touch with you."

"That's right good of you, love. You've taken a big weight off my mind. How's Madge? Is she keeping well?"

"Yes. She will be sorry to hear the news about your husband. I do hope he gets well soon."

Faint pips came over the line. "I must go now," Mrs. Lingard said hurriedly. "Tell Jim to ring any time tonight."

As Jenny replaced the receiver there was a knock at the door. She opened it and found Jim standing there.

"Can I come in, Jenny?' he asked.

"Oh, if only you had arrived a few minutes earlier," she cried. "Your mother has just phoned. Apparently your father is ill and she wants you to go home. You had better call her back."

His face fell. "Poor old Dad. I'd better see just how bad it is. Can I use your phone?"

"Of course," she said, and went into her bedroom to change into slacks and a sweater.

As she came back into the sitting-room, Jim put the receiver down, and turned to face her. He looked very worried.

"She says the doctor's been today and that Dad must stay in bed for some time," he said. "Evidently, it's his heart. He's been doing too much for a man of his age."

"Let's go into the kitchen and I'll make a cup of tea," Jenny suggested.

As she put the kettle on, Jim told her that he had come round to wait for Madge. He explained that, after he had stormed out of Miles Brent's office on the previous afternoon, he had been bitterly ashamed of himself.

"I went for a long walk to think things over, yesterday evening," he said. "I must have got lost in a maze of streets. I hadn't the nerve to come round when, eventually, I found my way. So I went home to bed."

"So you've come round to make things right with Madge now, is that it?" Jenny asked gently.

"That's about the size of it," he admitted. "I'm thoroughly ashamed of myself. I behaved badly — I let anger and jealousy blind me." He sighed. "I'm certainly out of luck at the moment. What do you think I ought to do about my father, Jenny?"

She met his eyes. Her usually laughing eyes were solemn.

"I think you ought to go home and shoulder your responsibilities, Jim," she said quietly.

"You mean, give up trying for success as an actor?"

"It depends how much that means to you, Jim. Somehow, I have a feeling that Hunsworth, your father and mother and the business, mean a great deal more to you than you're prepared to admit."

"I suppose you're right. It's one of the things I thought out during my long walk last night. I know now that I'm never going to make the grade on the stage or television. I was an idiot to believe that I ever could."

"Then — you'll go home?"

He nodded and got to his feet. He ran his hand through his shock of hair.

"Yes! I'll go and hire a car. There isn't a train that will get me to Hunsworth tonight. If I set off in the next hour or so, I can be home soon after midnight."

He turned and hurried towards the door. Suddenly he stopped and turned back to Jenny. "Thanks, Jenny, for being so understanding," he murmured affectionately. Jenny flushed and yearned to run to him and throw her arms about his neck. But she couldn't do that. He belonged to Madge.

"I'll tell Madge you called to see her, but that you had to go back to Hunsworth," she said, hoping that her inner turmoil was not apparent on her face.

He nodded. "I'll ring her as soon as I can," he said, then opened the door.

Jenny waited for the closing of the door to announce that he had gone out of her life forever; but it did not come. Instead, she heard Jim gasp, heard him exclaim: "Madge!"

Then she was across the room to the door and looking past Jim, where she saw Madge swaying in the doorway, her big eyes staring hopelessly out of her white face.

9

"**M**ADGE, what is it?"
Jim put his arm around her and led her into the flat.

Jenny went quickly forward. "Bring her to the fire, Jim," she said. "She's had a shock."

Soon they had Madge sitting before the electric fire, sipping Jenny's freshly-made tea. The colour came faintly back into her cheeks.

"Jim — Jenny — I'm sorry if I gave you a shock. I — I'm all right now."

"But what's happened to upset you so?" Jim demanded, with a perplexed frown.

"I'd rather not discuss it," she said hurriedly. "I — I shan't be going back to the office anymore."

Jim and Jenny exchanged a glance over Madge's head. Jim's eyes flashed.

"What has happened? You must tell me, Madge . . . " he began, but she shook her head.

"I don't want to talk about it yet." She turned to Jenny. "I think I'll go and lie down for a bit. My head's nearly splitting."

"Yes, do that," her friend agreed. "I'll bring you two aspirins when Jim's gone."

Madge looked at Jim. "Where are you going, Jim?" she asked. "Back to your flat?"

He shook his head. "No, Dad's ill. I must go back tonight, so I'm just going out to hire a car. I should reach Hunsworth shortly after midnight."

Her eyes lit up. Some of her lassitude seemed to leave her. She grabbed the sleeve of his jacket.

"Take me with you, Jim," she begged. "I can't stay in London — now."

"Well, I don't know . . . " he began uncertainly, but she hurried on:

"Please, Jim It's very important to

162

me. I — I never want to see London again."

"It will be a tiring drive. She doesn't look fit to do it, does she, Jenny?"

Jenny looked at her friend and saw, in Madge's face, a desperate appeal for her support. Some instinct told her that, perhaps, in spite of her friend's exhaustion, Madge would be better going with Jim than staying behind to face whatever had upset her.

"I think she'll be able to do it, Jim," she said. "After all, as you're going by car, she should be able to sleep most of the way."

"Oh, all right," Jim said. "And now I'd better try to hire a car. If we don't leave soon, we won't arrive in Hunsworth until the middle of the night. Perhaps you'd help Madge pack a few things, Jenny. I'll come back for her as soon as I can."

He made for the door and disappeared. Jenny looked down at Madge, who was staring blankly ahead of her.

"Oughtn't you to start getting ready,

Madge?" she asked gently. "There isn't much time."

Madge shivered suddenly, then glanced up at her friend.

"You must be wondering what has happened, Jenny," she whispered.

"I'll restrain my curiosity until you feel able to tell me," her friend said. "I'll go and get your suitcase. We haven't much time to pack, so let's just fling in the bare essentials, and I'll send on anything you may need, later."

Madge jumped up and suddenly hugged her. "Oh, Jenny, you are a good sort," she said, her voice breaking in a sob. "I'll always be grateful to you."

Jenny smiled at her. "Come on, dear, and let's get your things packed," she murmured. "You're going back home with the man you love. That means everything now. Nothing else matters."

As Madge sorted out the things she wanted to take with her, she began to feel better. Ever since she had rushed out of Miles's office and made her way home, she had felt frozen inside. Now the blood was beginning to course through her veins again. She was even beginning to want to talk about her awful experience.

She glanced at Jenny. What a wonderful friend she was! If only she could go back to Hunsworth as well. But Jenny would laugh at such a suggestion.

"I'm a Londoner now," she had often said. "I don't suppose I'll ever go back to live in Yorkshire."

"I'm sorry it had to end like this, Jenny," Madge said at last. "It's been wonderful, sharing this flat with you. I hope you get someone to take my place. It's too expensive for you to live here on your own."

"Oh, I'll manage," Jenny laughed, and felt glad that Madge did not suspect how her heart was aching at losing, in one fell swoop, the man she loved, and her best friend. Life was going to be very lonely in the coming weeks!

"I owe it to you to tell you what happened, before I go," Madge murmured, as she snapped the lock of the suitcase.

"You needn't tell me if you don't want to."

"I think I ought to. And I want to, anyway."

In an unsteady voice, more than once broken by sobs, she told her of the episode in Miles's office.

Jenny's face reddened with indignation as she listened.

"You — you mean they think you're a thief?" she gasped.

"Yes! I suppose it did look that way. After all, the bracelet was in my drawer. I was holding it in my hand when Miles and Pat came into the office."

"And that Carnford woman wanted to go to the police?"

"Yes, at first. I don't think she was so keen when Miles pointed out that it would cause a scandal."

"But who could have put the bracelet in your drawer?"

"I don't know. The whole thing's a — a mystery to me."

Jenny frowned. "Do you think you're wise to run away like this, Madge?"

"But I can't stay here, with everybody thinking me a thief. I shall tell Jim, on my way to Hunsworth, and if he, like you, believes in me, we shall be married and I'll never set foot in London again."

Jenny still looked doubtful but, as a heavy knock sounded at that moment, she said no more.

"That'll be Jim," Madge said, running out into the hall.

"I've got a car," Jim said, as she opened the door. "It's waiting in the street now. Are you ready?"

"Yes!" Madge took the case Jenny was holding out. "Good-bye, Jenny. I'll ring you, perhaps tomorrow evening."

"Good-bye, Madge!" Jenny kissed her warmly. "Have a good trip. And

— don't worry! I'm sure everything will come right in the end."

She stood at the top of the stairs, watching them go down to the street; then, her eyes blinded by sudden tears, she turned and went back into the lonely flat.

Out in the street, Jim put Madge's suitcase into the back of the car.

"It seems quite a good little bus," he said, as he helped her into the passenger seat. "We should reach Hunsworth soon after midnight."

As Jim started the car, Madge looked at him.

"Jim, I haven't said how sorry I am to hear of your father's illness," she said. "I suppose I was so taken up with my own affairs — "

"That's all right," he said, with a quick smile. "Mum and Dad will be thrilled to see you. They've a very soft spot for you, Madge."

She did not reply, but she was remembering how friendly Jim's people had always been when she had visited their house. They had seemed very disappointed when she had told them she was going to London and she was sure they would have preferred it if Jim had married her and kept her in Hunsworth.

Perhaps they believe that it's because of me that Jim came south, she thought. They might have decided he was following *me* to London — not a career on the stage. At any rate, he's going back now, so they'll be happy.

Jim said little as they drove through the London suburbs and took the main road north.

"Try to get a little sleep, Madge," he advised. "We'll stop for something to eat in a couple of hours. I don't suppose you've had a meal?"

She shook her head. Closing her eyes, she lay back in her corner; but at first she could not sleep. Her brain was too active. Over and over again, in her mind's eye, she saw Miles's amazed look as he came into the office and saw her, staring, as if hypnotized, at the bracelet she had found in her drawer. She heard again and again Pat's contemptuous voice urging him to get the police.

In their eyes, she was a thief. Only because Miles had not wanted a scandal had she been saved from being questioned by the police. She must stop thinking about it. She must stop thinking and relax.

After an hour or so, Jim's silence and the humming of the car engine lulled her into a doze.

Jim's voice awakened her. She opened her eyes to find that Jim had driven into a car park beside a brightly-lit transport café.

"This is where we eat," he said and, meeting her eyes, grinned. "Feel a bit better after your sleep? I'd have stopped before but you seemed well away and I decided to let you rest."

The clock on the dashboard said half-past nine.

"Oh, Jim," Madge cried, "you must be famished. Why did you wait so long? I wouldn't have minded being woken up."

Jim did not reply. He helped her from the car and across the car park to the long wooden building.

A gust of warmth and noise met them as they opened the door and went inside. A juke-box in the corner was blaring a Pop record; the voices of the men seated at the bare wooden tables rose to a roar above the music and the air was blue with tobacco smoke.

"Perhaps we should have gone on a bit farther and found something quieter," Jim said doubtfully as he looked around him.

But Madge shook her head. For some reason she felt quite at home in this bright, noisy place. Here there were too many distractions to allow her to sit and brood.

"No, let's stay here," she said. "There's a table for two over in that corner."

"What would you like to eat?" Jim asked, pulling out a chair for her.

Suddenly Madge felt ravenously hungry. Perhaps it was the sleep she had had, or the knowledge that London was now far away, that had revived her spirits.

"Bacon and eggs!" she replied promptly, and suddenly Jim smiled, a smile that warmed his grey eyes.

"That's my girl!" he said, and left her while he went across to the counter to give his order to the proprietor.

When he returned, he sat down opposite Madge and looked into her eyes. "You look a bit better," he declared. "Now I feel I can ask you to tell me what upset you this afternoon."

Madge hesitated. It was difficult to explain to anyone — even Jim — that she had been accused of dishonesty.

"I was accused of being a thief," she whispered at last.

Jim stared at her, incredulously. "You — you were accused of being a thief! But who accused you — and why?"

Madge felt the tears pricking her eyes

172

again. She said sadly, "I'll tell you the whole story."

She did so and, when she had finished, Jim sat in silence, looking very angry. For one dreadful moment Madge wondered if he, too, doubted her innocence. The story did seem incredible. Even as she was telling Jim, she had realized that.

A young waitress brought their plates of bacon, egg and chips. Jim began to eat in silence, and Madge stared at her plate and felt nauseated. The desire for food had gone as quickly as it had come.

Jim was thinking. He was remembering the previous day, when he had bumped into Patricia Carnford, and had hinted that Miles was in love with Madge.

Suppose she had been aroused to wreak vengeance upon Madge? Supposing she herself had put the bracelet in Madge's drawer.

There was no other explanation. He looked across the table and saw the white, stricken face of the girl at the other side. He stretched out his hand and laid it over hers.

"It sounds to me like a put-up job, Madge," he said. "I — I think I ought to tell you something."

He told her what he had said to Patricia. "She could easily have planted that bracelet in your drawer and written an anonymous letter to herself," he said.

"But how can I prove that?" Madge asked.

"I don't know that you can," he declared. "And now, eat your meal or it will get cold. And don't worry any more. I know you're not a thief — and so will everyone else who hears the story."

Madge's appetite returned, and she finished her meal with relish. Jenny believed in her, and so did Jim. She would close her mind for the time being to the thought of Miles and Patricia Carnford.

Later, as they drove on, Madge dozed again. When she awoke she saw that they had left the main road and were threading their way between rough stone walls, with trees and hedges silhouetted against the starry sky.

"Where are we, Jim?" she asked.

"We left the main road ten minutes ago," he replied. "I'm cutting across country. We should be in Hunsworth in half an hour or so."

"Good heavens!" Madge exclaimed. "Have I really been asleep for so long!"

She sat up straight and peered out of the window, watching the rows of grey stone cottages and the mill chimneys fly past. She felt suddenly glad to be home again. On a signpost she read *Hunsworth 7 miles*, and felt a thrill of anticipation. London, and all that had happened there, now seemed like a dream, and she was glad.

Jim turned to her, beaming. "Nearly home, Madge. I'm looking forward to seeing Mum's face — and Dad's, for that matter — when they see I've brought you home with me. They think the world of you."

They were soon driving through the centre of Hunsworth, and Madge watched eagerly for familiar places — the local cinema, where she and Jim had spent so much of their time; the library; the market place, shut up and deserted at this time of the night, but usually teeming with life.

They took a steep road beyond the town which led to the moors. Here were the houses of the better endowed citizens, most of them built in the grey local stone, about fifty years ago.

The iron gate of *Moor Croft* was closed. Jim jumped out and opened it, then drove up the short drive to the front of the big house. A light was burning behind the glass panels of the front door and another glowed behind the curtains of an upstairs room.

"That's Dad's room," Jim said, glancing up. "I dare say the front door will be unlocked, as they knew I was coming."

Madge got out of the car, and Jim

took her arm and led her to the steps that led up to the front door. His key turned easily in the lock, and he and Madge slipped into the wide hall.

A stout, rather dumpy figure, in a thick dressing-gown, plaited grey hair over one shoulder, appeared almost immediately at the top of the stairs.

She peered down at the two young people in the hall below. "Is that you, Jim?" Her voice was strained and, as she came down the stairs, Madge noticed the pallor of her cheeks and the shadows under her eyes.

Jim said, "You don't look too good yourself."

"Well, I've been sitting up with your father. He's pretty bad, this time, son. How glad I am that you've come home. And how nice of Madge to have come with you!"

"I do hope I'm not intruding, Mrs. Lingard," Madge said. "And how is Mr. Lingard?"

"The doctor came earlier this evening. He seems to think he's a bit better. Of course, knowing that you were coming has helped a lot, Jim."

She gave her son a hug, then turned towards Madge, arms held out. Her kind, homely face was shining with pleasure.

"Lovie, you must be tired out!" she cried, looking at Madge's pale face. "There's some hot soup in the kitchen, and I asked Ellen to cut some ham sandwiches. Let's go in there and warm ourselves up. It's a bit draughty in this hall. Then you can go and see Dad, Jim. He's sleeping now, but that won't last for long."

10

IT was a large kitchen with a red tiled floor, and a huge open grate. Mrs. Lingard went immediately to the fireplace to revive the dying fire. Then, when she had coaxed it into a good, healthy blaze, she settled Madge in a chair by the hearth.

"You drink that down, love," Mrs. Lingard said, handing a cup of steaming soup to Madge. "You look as if you could do with some nourishment. In fact, you don't look at all well. Is it the London air that's harmed you?"

Madge smiled, knowing that a reply was unnecessary, and sipped the hot soup. She felt the tenseness going out of her. How good it was to be 'home.' How different was the atmosphere of this old-fashioned Yorkshire home from the bright but brittle environment of the television world. How different was

Mrs. Lingard, with her simple, kindly ways, from the affected, self-seeking men and women who had drifted in and out of Miles Brent's office, day after day.

Jim was looking anxiously at his mother. "Mum, tell me frankly, what is wrong with Dad?"

She gave him a gentle, reassuring smile, which never-the-less did not belie the anxiety evident in her eyes. "He came home from work the other day, not feeling too well," she said quietly. "I persuaded him to have an early night, thinking a rest was all he needed. In the morning, though, when he got up as usual, he — he . . . "

Her voice faltered. Jim went quickly to her side and slipped his arm about her. "Now, now, Mum, it's all right," he comforted. "I'm here now. There's no need to worry any more."

His mother smiled bravely and patted his hand. "He had a dizzy spell, Jim, and I called the doctor," she said. "He ordered your father to bed and told me he'd had a heart attack. He needed complete rest. Of course, you know what your father's like. He said he'd be up and about again in a day or two and that he'd have to go back to the works, as there was no one to look after things now that you were in London."

"So you telephoned me?" Jim said. "You did right, Mum. I should never have gone away in the first place."

"There, there, love, how were you to know Dad would be taken ill? He's always been so strong."

"Well, I shall insist that Dad stays in bed just as long as it takes him to get well again. Can I go up and see him now, Mum?"

"Of course you can, dear. Perhaps Madge would like to go to bed. She looks tired out. Let me see! I'll put you in the back bedroom, love. Here, let me fill a hot water bottle for you and you can take it up with you."

Jim carried Madge's suitcase up to a bedroom at the end of the first floor landing. He switched on the electric fire and, with the curtains drawn against the night, the little room seemed very cosy and inviting.

"I hope you sleep well." Mrs. Lingard came to say good night and impulsively gave Madge a motherly kiss. "Stay in bed in the morning and I'll tell Ellen to bring you a breakfast tray."

"Oh, but — " Madge protested.

Jim laughed. "Don't you try to go against Mother. She's made up her mind that you're to have breakfast in bed, so you might as well accept the situation with as good a grace as you can muster!"

He kissed her, and mother and son left the room together. Madge unpacked a few things and then undressed and slipped into bed, hugging the hot water bottle.

It was a long time after she had slipped between the warm sheets that sleep came. Now that she was alone, she began to re-live again that scene in Miles's office. How it hurt her to remember, yet how impossible it was to forget. She felt cold all over and even the hot water bottle could not warm her.

When she did fall asleep, she slept heavily. She was awakened by someone pulling the curtains back and letting in a shaft of morning sunlight.

"Good morning, miss!" The tall, spare woman in a floral overall smiled at Madge. "I've got your tray outside the door. Mrs. Lingard told me to let you sleep until nine o'clock."

She put the tray across Madge's knees, and switched on the electric fire.

"Just ring if there's anything you want," she said and, with a cheerful smile, left the room.

Madge thoroughly enjoyed her breakfast of porridge, bacon and eggs and toast and marmalade. A little silver teapot supplied her with two large cups of tea.

I'm living in the lap of luxury, she thought. Very different from the rush and scramble at the flat every morning.

Remembering how Jenny would, by this time, have dashed off to work, she felt a little sad. She had enjoyed sharing the flat with her friend. Jenny was a wonderful person to live with — tolerant, kind, always cheerful.

Well, that was all over now. She would not be returning to London. In future, her life was based here, in Hunsworth — with Jim.

When she was dressed she went downstairs and met Mrs. Lingard in the hall.

"Ah, there you are, love," the older woman said. "Did you sleep well?"

"Yes, thank you," Madge replied. "How is Mr. Lingard this morning?"

"Much better for seeing Jim, I can tell you! He had his first good night's sleep for a long time."

"I'm so glad. I suppose Jim has gone to the works?"

"Yes, he was off by eight o'clock. That's another thing that pleased his father." She hesitated, then added: "By the way, Mr. Lingard would very much like to see you, Madge. He's been asking after you."

"I'd very much like to see him," Madge said.

"Then there's no time like the present," Mrs. Lingard smiled. "Follow me, love."

As she followed Mrs. Lingard's stout form up the wide staircase, Madge wondered what Jim's father wanted to say to her.

Would he assume, as she had come north with his son, that she was to many Jim in the very near future? Well, she could always say, if he questioned her, that Jim had not yet asked her.

Mrs. Lingard opened a door at the top of the stairs and peered around it. "Yes, he's awake," she whispered to Madge, and beckoned her to follow her into the bedroom.

"Here's Madge to see you, Dad!" she cried, and Madge saw he was propped against pillows in a big double bed.

She was shocked at the change in him. He had been a robust, well-built man. Now he looked pathetically frail, sitting up in the big double bed. His once bright eyes were sunken, and his skin looked paper-thin. He smiled faintly at Madge and held out his hand.

"It's nice to see you, Madge," he said. "Come and sit beside me."

To her relief, he talked of London and her life there, and hardly mentioned Jim. But she had a feeling that he was watching her, as if wondering about the real purpose of her visit to Hunsworth. She told him of her work at Metropolitan Television, wondering, as she did so, how he would react if she mentioned the circumstances in which she had left her job.

"Jim tells me he's appeared in a play," he said. "I was sorry his mother felt she ought to send for him on my account, just when he was on the verge of making a success in his new profession."

It was on the tip of Madge's tongue to reveal to him that Jim had not proved to be a success, but she decided that this was not her right. It was up to Jim himself to tell his father that he had made a mistake. He might not want to; might decide to let his father go on believing that he had thrown up a promising career for his sake. That would please his parents and save his pride.

After a few minutes Mrs. Lingard, who had been standing by the window, came over to the bed.

"I think that's long enough for a first visit," she said. "Dad soon tires, Madge. Perhaps you'll look in on him again later?"

"Of course I will!" Madge smiled down at the elderly man. "It's nice of you to let me stay here, Mr. Lingard."

"You're welcome, my dear." Just for a moment he took her hand and pressed it. "I hope you'll stay a long time, a very long time indeed."

As she followed Mrs. Lingard from

the room, Madge knew what Mr. Lingard had been trying to convey: that he hoped she and Jim would marry soon and live permanently at *Moor Croft*.

* * *

After Madge had left with Jim, Jenny did some thinking.

But it's nonsense that anyone should ever think Madge was a thief! she told herself indignantly. Gosh, I'd like to have that Miles Brent here at this moment. I'd tell him a thing or two — "

She sat down at the table and began to eat her supper. Sudden inspiration came to her and she stopped eating, fork poised half-way to her mouth.

Why shouldn't I tell him what I think of him? He's here in London, isn't he?

She hurried through her meal, stacked the washing-up in the sink, then went to the telephone and picked up the telephone directory.

It didn't take long to find Miles's number. All she had to do was lift the receiver and, when Miles answered, let fly at him.

Then she read the address printed after his name in the directory. It shouldn't be too difficult to find.

Why shouldn't she go to see him in person? If she merely telephoned, he could hang up before she had said all she wanted to. How much better could she show her anger of his treatment of Madge if she had him standing before her!

With Jenny, an idea like that led to instant action. Hurrying into her bedroom, she pulled on her coat and, two minutes later, was hurrying down the stairs to the street.

Her indignation lasted until the bus she took put her down two streets from the block of flats in which Miles lived. But, as she approached the big building, she was filled with apprehension. Miles was an important man. What right had she, a plain unimportant secretary, to reprimand him, whatever he had done?

Go home, she urged herself. You're only going to make a fool of yourself. No one knows you've come here, so no one will ever know that you backed out at the last minute.

Then she remembered how distraught Madge had been, and again she was filled with indignation. Fired by this indignation she marched into the block of flats, summoned the lift, and was soon standing outside Miles's front door.

She put her finger on the bell push and held it there.

At first there was no response; then she heard approaching footsteps from within and a man's voice saying: "All right, I'm coming!" The door was opened and Jenny found herself face to face with Miles Brent.

For a moment he frowned, as if not recognizing her; then he smiled. "Hello there! You're Madge's friend, Jenny, aren't you?"

She nodded. "Yes, I am! I would like a word with you, please, Mr. Brent."

"You'd better come in," he said, and stood aside so that she could go forward into the hall.

"Who is it, darling?"

As Miles closed the door Patricia Carnford came out of a room on the right. She frowned, seeing Jenny.

"You may remember that Miss Briggs and Madge share a flat," Miles said.

"We did," Jenny said bluntly. "Madge left London this evening."

"She left London this evening!" Miles repeated, and Jenny was surprised at the dismay in his voice.

"Yes, that's why I've come to see you," Jenny said sharply. "I understand that this afternoon you accused my friend of being a thief, Mr. Brent!"

Before Miles could speak, his fiancée said angrily: "She *is* a thief! I suppose she didn't tell you that Mr. Brent and I caught her with my missing diamond bracelet in her hand."

"No, Pat — " Miles began, but

Pat was obviously determined that he should not have his say.

"She must have found the bracelet and hidden it in her drawer," she went on. "She wasn't expecting my fiancé and me to come in while she was examining it."

"Someone else put the bracelet in her drawer," Jenny cried. "Anyone with any sense would know that Madge is incapable of stealing anything from anyone. Mr. Brent," Jenny turned to Miles. "You must know that Madge is innocent."

"Is that why your precious friend has cleared out of London?" Patricia Carnford sneered, before Miles could reply. "If that isn't proof of her guilt, I don't know what is!"

"Madge was so disgusted by the mistrust of people who should have believed in her," Jenny glanced with contempt at Miles, "that all she wanted was to get away, to go back home to the north and forget her horrible experience."

"A likely tale!"

Miles stood watching them, looking very embarrassed. For the first time in several minutes he spoke. "I think it would be a good idea if we all cooled down," he said, and went into the sitting-room, followed by Jenny and Patricia. When the three were settled in armchairs around the fire he said: "First, I want to make it clear that I did not accuse Madge of being a thief. In fact, I think the whole thing is a most unfortunate mistake."

"How can it be a mistake?" his fiancée demanded. "And are you forgetting the anonymous letter I received?"

"No, I'm not forgetting that, but it does not prove Madge's guilt. It may very well have been written by some spiteful person who wanted to hurt Madge."

"But what on earth for? People who do things like that must have some motive for their actions? What could

193

anyone gain by making Madge appear a thief?"

"I wonder," Jenny said softly, and her eyes were on the beautiful face of the girl sitting beside Miles.

"Do you expect Madge to come back to London?" Miles asked.

"I don't know. She may never come back again," Jenny said quietly.

"Because she dare not, I suppose," Patricia sneered. "She knows very well that, if I changed my mind and preferred a charge against her, she might find herself going before the magistrates."

"Don't talk like that, Pat!" Miles protested. "It's very understandable that Madge should go home for a bit — "

Before he could say more, Jenny, her freckled face flaming, stood up and walked over to where Patricia was sitting. Patricia shrank back, as if she thought Jenny was about to hit her, but Jenny contented herself with a verbal attack.

"If you don't know goodness when you see it, I'm sorry for you," she cried. "Madge is pure gold, as I've had reason to know during the years I've been her best friend. Anyone who tries to blacken her character is a contemptible creature. You're a nasty piece of work, Miss Patricia Carnford, and it's time someone told you so. You asked, a few minutes ago, who would gain by making Madge out to be a thief. Well, that's obvious to me, if it isn't to your fiancé. I think, if he cared to look for the writer of the anonymous letter, he might find the spiteful person who also put the bracelet in Madge's drawer. I don't think he need look any farther than this room!"

Patricia's mouth gaped open. For once, she was lost for words. Miles got to his feet. "Now, Miss Briggs, can't we discuss this quietly?"

"Nothing is to be gained from further discussion," Jenny replied. "Good night."

There was silence in the room after

the slam of the front door announced that she had gone.

"Of all the dreadful things to say!" Patricia said, a sob in her voice and a cautious glance in Miles's direction.

He did not speak for a few seconds but contented himself with taking a cigarette from a box on the table and lighting it. He had his back turned to her.

"Miles," Patricia began nervously. "What are you thinking about? Why are you so silent, darling?"

Miles turned to face her. "Pat, I've just had an idea," he said. "It occurs to me that there's a very easy way of finding out whether Madge put the bracelet in the drawer or not."

She frowned. What did he mean?

"I — I don't quite follow, Miles," she murmured.

"Why, all I need to do is to call in a finger-print expert," he said quietly. "If there are only Madge's finger-prints and yours on the bracelet, then Madge must have taken it. If there are no

196

finger-prints in Madge's drawer but her own, then that again would prove her guilt. But we must be sure, Patricia."

She felt her heart sink.

"But if the expert finds any finger-prints that aren't Madge's, I mean — how will you discover whose they really are?"

He shrugged. "Well, I can ask the people who are known to have visited my office to have their finger-prints taken, for a start. That will eliminate quite a few from the list."

He gave her a sharp glance. "You wouldn't mind having your prints taken, would you, Pat?" he asked.

She gave a nervous little laugh. "Why, of course not! Why should I?" she cried.

"Then that's settled. I'll arrange for an expert to get to work first thing in the morning. And now, what about going out to eat? I'm starving, and too lazy to cook a meal myself."

Patricia put her hand to her head and sighed. "I think I'd rather go home, if you don't mind, Miles," she said. "I've got a dreadful headache. The only thing I want to do right now is to sink into bed."

He was instantly all concern. "I'll run you home," he said, but she shook her head.

"I'll pick up a taxi outside," she said. "Please don't bother, Miles. You go and get yourself something to eat."

"But I can't let you go off like this — " he protested. "It won't take me long to run you home, and then I'll eat."

"Oh, all right," she said ungraciously. "I thought I'd save you the bother, but if you insist, why should I complain?"

Pat said little on the short journey to her flat, which was not very far away.

"How's the headache now?" Miles asked, as he helped her out of the car outside her block of flats.

"Worse than ever," she said — and, with a wan little smile, added: "I won't ask you up, darling. As soon as I get in, I'm going to have a hot bath and go straight to bed."

"I hope you'll feel better in the morning," Miles said. "Sleep tight." Pat nodded, and then turned and hurried across the pavement. When she had gone Miles slid behind the wheel again and drove down the street.

At the corner he turned left and parked. Getting out of the car he went to look cautiously along the other street again. He had been standing there less than two minutes when he saw Pat come out into the street again, looking anxiously up and down. Then she waved frantically to an approaching taxi.

As I expected, he thought grimly, as he watched her climb into the cab.

A minute later he had turned his car and was starting off along the street, with the rear light of the taxi winking through the darkness several yards ahead.

11

AS Miles followed the taxi through the lamp-lit streets his mind was in a turmoil. So much seemed to have happened. Much that had confused and bewildered him.

First, there had been that terrible moment when he and Pat had walked into his office and found Madge with the bracelet in her hand. He did not believe for one moment that Madge could have stolen it; he knew her well enough to realize that she was incapable of such mean action. Yet things had happened so quickly. Patricia had been ruthless and harsh with Madge, and Madge had fled in fear. Yes, that was why she had run away — not because she was guilty, but because she was afraid. She had been put in an intolerable position, and he had done nothing to help her. Yet, what could he have done. Surely he owed first loyalty to Patricia?

Patricia? Was he in love with her? Somehow he did not think he was. Not very long ago she had seemed to be the most wonderful girl in the world, but just lately he had begun to wonder if he might not perhaps he dazzled by her beauty and infatuated by her vivacity. An hour ago, when Jenny had hinted that it was Pat who had planted the bracelet on Madge, he should have been immediately angry that someone was trying to blacken his fiancée's reputation. Instead, he had found himself wondering whether it could possibly be so. Surely that was not the reaction of a man in love?

Yet why should Pat want to ruin Madge? he asked himself. What motive could she have? Jealousy? Jealous of what? Then he knew! He loved Madge — had loved her for some time — and Pat had realized this, and had determined to get her rival out of the way.

What a blind fool I've been! Miles thought. How Madge must be hating me!

As the taxi which had been heading north, turned suddenly to the left, Miles knew that his hunch had been right. In a few moments, the huge building which housed the Metropolitan Television Company would come into sight.

Suddenly Miles braked hard. The taxi ahead was drawing to a halt at the pavement. He must not be seen by Pat. Naturally, she would not drive up to the front entrance of the building where she would almost certainly be recognized. Her plan would be to pay the taxi driver and enter by a back door.

There was a side street nearby and, as Pat stepped from the taxi, Miles drove into this street. It led between high walls to another street, a hundred yards ahead — which, in turn, came out into the main road opposite the television headquarters. Half a minute later, he was parking his car and making for the brightly-lit main entrance.

"Good evening, Mr. Brent!"

The commissionaire saluted as he hurried past. By the lift he glanced back. There was no sign of Pat.

The lift took him up to his floor. Near his office there was a door which led to the fire escape. He slipped through this, leaving it open perhaps an inch. In this way, he could keep his office under observation and no one would be able to enter or leave it without his seeing them.

For some time nothing happened. The office staff had long since gone home and this part of the big building was silent and empty.

Miles glanced at his watch. What was keeping Pat? It was nearly a quarter of an hour since he had seen her get out of the taxi.

Then, he heard the sound of footsteps coming along the corridor. He leaned forward, peering through the crack in the door.

He saw Pat stealing furtively along the corridor, and held his breath as she put out her hand and turned the handle of the office door.

A moment later the corridor was empty again.

Miles waited. His heart was thundering. Every instinct urged him to go forward and fling open the office door. But he knew that, if he appeared a moment too early, Pat might be able to find an excuse. No! he must catch her red-handed, actually trying to remove the finger-prints from inside the drawer.

At last, he emerged from his hiding-place and crept towards his office door. What he had to do was distasteful, but he knew there could be no shirking of his responsibilities. Madge's — his own — happiness depended on what he did in the next few seconds.

Slowly and noiselessly he turned the door handle. He saw Pat before she saw him. She had turned on the light after pulling the curtains over the window, and was standing at Madge's desk. She had the drawer open and was busily wiping the inside.

Then she looked up and saw him watching her from the doorway. "Miles!" she gasped and her face was ashen. "What are you doing here?"

"I thought you'd come back," he said, closing the door and walking towards her.

When she did not speak, he went on: "It was you who put the bracelet in the drawer, wasn't it, Pat? That story you told me about losing it was a lie."

"I — I — " She stammered, helplessly. "You — you've no right to say such a thing. I . . . "

"I've every right!" His voice was full of contempt. "How could you do such a thing, Pat? If I hadn't followed you tonight there'd have been no way of clearing Madge's name."

Suddenly Patricia went wild. Perhaps it was the look of scorn on Miles's face that sparked off her fury; perhaps it was the knowledge that now she had lost him forever, the man she had fought so desperately to keep.

"Do you think I cared whether her name was ever cleared or not?" she shouted, her voice rising hysterically. "I could see she was trying to steal you from me and I was determined she shouldn't. You're mine, Miles, not hers. I made up my mind to get rid of her any way I could."

"So you admit you put the bracelet in her drawer?"

"Of course I admit it! What's the good of denying it now? And I'm not sorry I did it. If it hadn't been for that other girl's visit, I would have got away with it. It was she who put it into your head that it might be me, wasn't it?"

"Yes, it was, though I would probably have got around to thinking it out for myself in time."

"But you'd never have been able to prove it. With the finger-prints wiped away — "

"I doubt if you'd have left any finger-prints on that rough wood," he told her, a little wearily. "I wasn't serious about calling in a finger-print expert. I just wanted to see how you would react. After I had dropped you at the flat, I hung around and saw you get into the taxi. I followed you here."

Suddenly Pat's shoulders slumped, her anger left her, and she began to sob like a child. She reached out to grasp Miles by the arm, but he shook her off. His eyes were hard and unrelenting.

"Miles, can't you understand? I love you. I only did it because — because I was afraid of losing you."

"It's no good, Pat," Miles said slowly. "I can never forgive you for what you've done to Madge. If you've any decency you'll write her a letter, apologizing for the pain you've caused her."

She stared at him through her tears as if he had taken leave of his senses.

"Me — apologize!" she gasped. "No, I'd rather die. I don't feel sorry, Miles. How dare she try to take you from me!" She pushed herself closer to him, and tried to stroke his face. "She hasn't succeeded, has she, darling? You are still mine, aren't you? We'll be married soon, won't we?"

Miles looked at her in disgust, and pushed her away.

It was the final insult to Pat. Tears coursing down her cheeks, she ran from the room.

Miles allowed her a few minutes to get out of the building, and then went down to his car and sat at the wheel, deep in thought.

Somehow, he must let Madge know that her name was cleared. He must go to Jenny's flat and get Madge's address from her.

He started the engine and drove into the main road. Somewhere near at hand a clock struck the half-hour. If he made straight for Jenny's flat he should be able to catch her before she went to bed.

He recollected sadly how, not very long ago, he had driven this way with Madge by his side. That was the night she had taken him up to the flat and introduced him to Jenny. If only he had known then what he knew now, he would have saved them both a great deal of unhappiness. But then he had thought himself in love with Pat. And there was still Jim Lingard to consider. Because he, Miles, loved Madge, it did not mean that Madge loved him. She had made it pretty obvious that she intended to settle down with Jim, someday. No, he knew that he loved in vain, and yet he must let her know that her innocence had been proved.

Jenny was very surprised to see Miles.

"Can I come in for a minute, Jenny?" he asked. "I have something to say that I'm sure will interest you."

Rather reluctantly she stepped aside. She was wearing a dressing-gown and her red hair, which she had been brushing when Miles rang, hung about her shoulders.

"I was just going to bed," she said, as he followed her into the sitting-room.

"What I have to say won't take more than a few minutes," he promised.

"I've come to tell you that Madge's innocence has been proven beyond doubt. I set a trap and the culprit fell into it!"

She listened quietly as he explained.

"I want you to tell me where Madge is, Jenny," he said at last. "The sooner she knows about this, the better!"

Her green eyes were cold as they met his. "You should never have doubted her, Mr. Brent, as I said earlier this evening!" she declared icily. "Whatever the evidence, I, for one, would never have believed Madge could do anything underhand or dishonest."

"I didn't believe it, either," he protested. "It was just that — "

"There is no excuse for the way you behaved!" she cried. "You let her come home, shocked, frightened, and very upset that you could have thought her guilty of theft. If I hadn't come round to see you tonight — "

"I know, I was wrong," he admitted quietly. "I should have had the courage of my convictions; but, at the time, I was too amazed to do anything. I had no reason to suspect my fiancée at that time."

With a weary shrug Jenny turned away. It was obvious that she considered the visit at an end.

But Miles made no move to leave.

"I want Madge's address," he said in a low voice.

Jenny swung round on him and her green eyes were flashing.

"And I don't feel inclined to give it to you. Why can't you leave the poor girl alone? I'll tell her what you've said. It seems to me all you're concerned about is easing your own conscience by letting her know you no longer think her a thief!"

"That's not true! I want to apologize to her for even doubting her for a single second."

She took a step towards him. "Why don't you leave Madge alone?" she demanded. "She's gone back home with the man she loves, the man she's going to marry. Why should

211

you, just to ease your conscience, start interfering? I'll tell Madge all she needs to know. She said she might telephone me tomorrow."

It was on the tip of Miles's tongue to tell Jenny that he knew he loved Madge, that he wanted to ask her to be his wife. Then he knew that was impossible. As Jenny had pointed out, Madge had gone home with the man she loved . . .

"So she is going to marry Jim Lingard?" he asked.

Jenny turned her head away so that he would not see the pain in her eyes.

"Of course she is! They've gone to Hunsworth to see Jim's mother and father. Mr. Lingard is ill and they both felt their place was with — "

He smiled faintly. "So, after all, Jenny, you've told me where Madge is! Now I must be off. Please tell Madge, when she rings you, what happened this evening. And tell her that I'm going to miss her. Good night!"

He hurried to the door and out into the hall. She looked after him, a strange expression on her face. Something in Miles's voice had told her the truth. He loved Madge. And now that love was as hopeless as her own secret love for Jim.

When she heard the door close behind him, she sank into a chair and buried her face in her hands.

12

JIM was sitting in his father's chair in the office at the printing works. Looking round the little room, with its old-fashioned roll-top desk, its filing cabinet and its huge portrait of Jim's grandfather, he drew a deep breath of pleasure.

He wondered why he had never felt like this before. Perhaps it was because his father had always made the decisions, ruled the roost from this small office which overlooked the works below. Until today Jim had been little more than one of the workmen who ran the big printing presses. Rarely had his father taken him into his confidence or made him feel that someday the works would be his to run in his own way.

Now, because of his father's illness, he was the boss. It was unlikely his father would ever be as strong as he had been, which meant that from now on the responsibility of running the business would be mainly his. True, he would ask his father's advice, but if there were any problems to solve, the final decision would be his — at least, until his father was on his feet again.

Already, since he had come to the office, an hour before, his advice had been sought by old Tomkins, the works foreman. Tomkins had seemed relieved to have someone to pour out his troubles to, and Jim had gathered that, for same time now, his father had been off colour, not able to deal with business matters quite as briskly and efficiently as before.

Miss Jenkins, too, who had been his father's secretary for nearly twenty years, told him, after she had asked after the elder Mr. Lingard, that she was delighted he had taken over.

"Things have been getting very neglected in the last month or so, Mr. Lingard," she said, her round, plain face shining with pleasure to see him established behind his father's desk. "I'm sure you'll make a big difference. Not that I'm saying anything against your father, mind, but he hasn't been well for some time. Even before you went off to London he complained of feeling tired."

"Did he?" Jim said. "I didn't know that."

"You were always so keen on your outside interests, Mr. Lingard," Miss Jenkins murmured reproachfully. "I often told your father he should give you more responsibility, but he used to say you weren't interested."

Jim had felt a stab of remorse on hearing this. It was true enough. He had acted very selfishly. He had worked beside his father day by day, not realizing that he needed his help. Ah, well, that was all over now. He had come back to Hunsworth and here he meant to stay.

As he worked, he found himself thinking of Madge. He supposed his mother and father would expect him to get married soon. He had never actually proposed to Madge, but it had always been taken for granted that one day they would marry.

Tonight he had better speak to her. If she agreed there was no reason why they shouldn't be married in a matter of weeks. He did not feel exhilarated by the idea. Why? He loved Madge, didn't he? Yes, he did; but why were his thoughts full of Jenny; dear, kind Jenny, with her pleasant face and beautiful smile?

He remembered that it had been to Jenny he had gone when he was worried and unhappy about getting a job in London. It was Jenny, not Madge, who had helped him when he had to decide about the flat. It had been Jenny who, when his father was taken ill, had pointed out that it was his duty to return home. He had come to value her good opinion.

That afternoon, he went through the works. The thunder of the machines shook the old building, and they seemed to fill the air with a definite rhythm.

"Jen-ny! Jen-ny!" they were saying and Jim stood, transfixed, as the truth burst on him like a bombshell.

It was Jenny he loved, not Madge. It was with Jenny that he wanted to spend his life, to have her always by his side, advising, consoling and loving. He was sure she was capable of great love.

As he drove back to *Moor Croft* that evening he made his decision. But first he would talk things over with his mother. He had great faith in her commonsense. She would have Madge's happiness at heart as well as his own.

To his relief, Madge was nowhere in sight when he entered the house.

He made straight for the little sewing-room at the back of the house. If his mother was not upstairs in his father's bedroom she would be in her favourite retreat. He hoped that Madge would not be with her.

Fortunately, his mother was alone.

She looked up from her work as he entered. "Ah, there you are, Jim!" she smiled. "Have you had a good day at the works?"

"Yes, thanks!" He crossed the room, and dropped a kiss on her soft hair. "Where's Madge?"

"Upstairs with your father. She volunteered to read the paper to him. She's a good girl, Jim."

Jim sat down at the other side of the fireplace. "It was about Madge I wanted to talk to you, Mum," he said slowly.

She took off her spectacles and beamed across at him.

"Have you finally made up your mind to marry her, then, Jim?" she asked eagerly.

"I want your opinion, Mum," he said. "Oh, I know you think I've been in love with Madge for a long time, and that it's time I asked her to become engaged to me. But — "

Her kindly face wore an anxious look. "So there's a 'but,' is there, love?" she murmured. "Well, you had better tell me what it's all about."

It came out with a rush, then. How he had found he loved Jenny, not Madge; what a wonderful girl Jenny was, but how he hated hurting Madge, who had always believed he loved her . . .

His voice died away. Mrs. Lingard looked into the fire for nearly half a minute before she spoke. "And you want me to advise you what to do, is that it, Jim?" she asked at last. "Well, I can't tell you who to marry, son. That decision is entirely your own."

"Yes, I know that, Mum, and I have decided that I shall ask Jenny to marry me. What I want to know is how to break the news to Madge."

Mrs. Lingard smiled sadly. "You are bound to cause her a lot of unhappiness at first, Jim, but everything will sort itself out, I'm sure. After all, you won't be much good to her if you don't love her. Better for her to know now."

"What do you think I should say then?"

"I should tell her exactly what you have told me. Tell her you've found out that you love Jenny and that you don't feel it would be right, in those circumstances, to marry her. I'm sure she will understand."

* * *

Madge had had a busy day. That morning, after helping with the housework, she had gone into Hunsworth to do the shopping. She had enjoyed walking through the familiar streets, basket over her arm. She had met several old friends who had stopped for a chat and it had been lunch-time when she had returned to *Moor Croft*.

I suppose it will be like this when Jim and I are married, she thought, and suddenly — quite without reason — she wondered how Miles was managing without her. He had always said she made life so easy for him.

"I'd be lost if you stayed away for even a couple of days," he had once said.

But she had to put him out of her mind. Miles obviously cared nothing for her. He still believed her to be a thief.

In the afternoon, she helped Ellen in the kitchen; and then, after a cup of tea, took old Spot, Jim's dog, for a short walk. When she had returned to the house she had relieved Mrs. Lingard in the sick room and had sat with Jim's father, even after he had fallen asleep.

As she came downstairs she found Jim waiting for her in the hall.

"Jim!" She seemed very pleased to see him. "Have you had a good day?"

He took her arm and led her towards the sitting-room. "I want to talk to you, Madge," he said.

A sense of panic overcame her. Was Jim going to propose — now? And if he did, what would she reply? Perhaps she could say she'd like to think things over. But he might point out that, as they'd been virtually engaged for over a year, she should have made up her mind by this time.

He closed the sitting-room door and joined her by the fire. She noticed that he looked uneasy, and supposed he was as nervous as she was.

"What is it, Jim?" she asked, when he did not speak.

"It — it's awfully hard to put into words, Madge," he muttered — and, to gain time, he got out a cigarette and lit up. "You see, I — I've always thought that one day we — might get married. You were my girl. I — I've never thought about anyone else until — "

She frowned, puzzled. What was he trying to tell her? That he didn't love her, after all?

"Go on, Jim?" she whispered.

He looked into her eyes for the first time, and his hand came out and clasped hers.

"I'm trying to tell you that — that I've found I don't love you, Madge," he said wretchedly. "When I brought you to Hunsworth last night I meant to ask you to marry me, as soon as possible; but — but today I realized something I didn't know before . . . "

"That you love Jenny?" Madge asked softly.

He dropped her hand in amazement. "How did you guess?" he gasped.

"It must have been at the back of my mind for quite a long time," she said. "I suppose I knew in my heart that Jenny had fallen in love with you — "

"You knew *that*!"

"Subconsciously, perhaps, but now I know it is so. And more than once, in London, you seemed to turn to Jenny rather than to me."

"I feel rotten about it, Madge," he muttered.

"You needn't!" She smiled at him. "As a matter of fact, Jim, when you were waiting in the hall and said you had something to say to me, I was wondering how I could put you off for a while, if you proposed. I don't

love you, Jim. I only thought I did
— once."

He smiled back, still looking at her
a little uncertainly.

"You're quite sure it's all right?"

She nodded. Standing on tip-toe,
she kissed his cheek. "I hope we'll
always be good friends, Jim," she said
— then, suddenly, turned and ran from
the room.

She was half-way upstairs, on the way
to her bedroom, when the telephone in
the hall rang. Ellen, the maid, who was
carrying a tray to the dining-room, went
to answer it.

"It's for you, miss," she said to
Madge, who paused, wondering whether
she should answer the phone.

Madge frowned. Who could be
telephoning her?

"Yes?" she said, taking the receiver.

"It's me — Jenny!" the voice at the
other end declared.

"Jenny! How wonderful to hear from
you! I was going to phone you very
soon."

"Madge, listen! I've got something very important to tell you." Jenny was obviously excited.

"What is it, Jenny?"

"I haven't had a chance to phone you all day, but this is the first thing I've done since I got in. It's about the bracelet you were accused of stealing!"

Madge's heart gave a lurch. So she hadn't finished with that distasteful subject yet! Perhaps — perhaps Patricia Carnford had persuaded Miles to call in the police, after all.

She waited in silence. Jenny, at the other end, cried: "Are you still there, Madge?"

"Yes, I'm here. What do you want to tell me, Jenny?"

"Miles Brent came to see me last night. It seems he has discovered that his darling fiancée planted the bracelet in your drawer!"

"But — but how did he find out?"

Jenny proceeded to tell her the story, with many indignant exclamations. "I must admit, though, that he showed a certain amount of low cunning in making her give herself away," she chuckled. "He came to see me, and asked me to pass on the good news!"

"Thanks, Jenny," Madge said dully. "I — I suppose he couldn't have told me himself."

Jenny drew a deep breath. "I didn't think you'd want to talk to him," she said. "He shouldn't ever have suspected you in the first place. I told him you wouldn't want him to seek you out, as you were getting married to Jim."

"But I'm not!" Madge almost shouted the words over the phone. It seemed so awful that Jenny had prevented Miles from contacting her. Miles — the one person she really wanted to see.

"What's that?" Jenny demanded. "Did I hear you say you weren't marrying Jim, after all?"

"Yes, you did! And there's a very good reason."

"Can't you tell me what it is?"

"No, I can't. But I have a feeling you'll hear all about it very soon."

Quietly she replaced the receiver, and went slowly upstairs. Life seemed to have come to a standstill for her. Her future was no longer in Jim's hands. She now had nothing to tie her to this part of the country — and yet she could not, would not, return to London. For the first time in her life she was utterly alone.

The following morning, while Mrs. Lingard and Ellen were busy about the house, Madge took Spot for a walk on the moors behind *Moor Croft*.

It was a glorious day, with fleecy-white clouds hanging high in a deep blue sky. The bright sun sparkled on a dozen moorland tarns, turning them into gleaming jewels among the purple heather.

Madge strode out, with Spot plodding some yards behind her. Today must be her last day of freedom. Tomorrow, she must start looking for a job, even if only a temporary one. For the time being, she would remain in Hunsworth. It shouldn't be too difficult to find something to do. Secretaries with her qualifications were in great demand.

Against her will, she imagined herself back at Metropolitan Television, working beside Miles. What an interesting job it had been and how considerate an employer was Miles.

She mustn't think of Miles. He had gone out of her life forever. But, although she tried to shut him out of her thoughts, he always returned. She found herself speculating about Patricia Carnford. Surely she and Miles were not still engaged. Miles must have been appalled at his fiancée's vicious attempt to blacken his secretary's name.

She supposed he would bury himself in his work, in the future. He was the sort of man who, after being badly hurt, would not lay himself open to a similar experience ever again.

Madge was so deep in her thoughts that she did not particularly notice the direction she was taking. Suddenly, her foot, as she placed it on what appeared to be a firm tussock, sank beneath her.

She fell forward, putting out her hands to break the fall. She tried to struggle to her feet but, to her terror, felt herself sinking into the bog. Fear overcame her, and she began to cry for help.

But only Spot, the Lingards' old dog, stood at the edge of the marshy ground, staring at her with helpless eyes.

"This is stupid!" Madge spoke aloud, in order to calm herself. "I've nothing to worry about. If I keep my head, I'll be out of here in a minute. I mustn't panic. I must not panic!"

Yet she could not forget the stories she had heard of other travellers lost on these wastes. They had been seen to leave the road, then never heard of again . . .

She had to get out before she sank any farther into the bog. Now, the soft mud was gripping her waist . . .

"Help! Help!"

In desperation, she cried out, hoping against hope that some shepherd, tending his sheep, might hear her faint shout.

A man, climbing from the road, quickened his pace as he heard the call. He had seen Madge heading up to the moor, with Spot plodding behind. He had stopped his car at the side of the road and had set off to catch her up.

Spot was the first to see him. He gave a joyful bark and ran to meet the newcomer.

"Hold on, Madge!" the man cried. "Try not to struggle. I'll soon have you on dry land again."

His voice penetrated her petrified brain. Miles! But that was ridiculous. Miles was in London.

She had her back to him, so she did not see him lie, face downwards, on the moss and edge slowly forward until his hands could reach out to grasp her arms.

"Lie back, as if you were floating in a swimming bath," he murmured. "I'm going to pull for all I'm worth."

She did as he told her. Gradually, she felt herself being drawn from the grip of the morass. A couple of feet behind her she heard Miles's heavy breathing as he strained to draw her towards him.

At last she was lying, mud-bespattered, on the firmer ground. Miles knelt beside her, and gazed anxiously into her eyes. Spot began to lick her face with a rough, moist tongue.

"So this is the sort of thing you get up to when I'm not around," Miles said softly.

"I — I — " Madge began, then suddenly burst into tears, her whole body shaking with the violence of her emotion.

"There, there, it's all right now," he said. "Come on, put your arms around my neck and I'll carry you to the car."

She stopped crying and allowed herself to be lifted up in his strong, gentle arms. How good it was to rest her head against his shoulder, to feel his arms about her. The nightmare had suddenly become a wonderful dream — or so it seemed. She did not want to ask questions, she only wanted to be still and quiet — but she had to know.

"But how did you come to be here, Miles? I — I thought you were in London."

"Jenny rang me last night. She thought I might like to know that you weren't going to marry Jim Lingard after all, and she gave me your address."

"But — but why should she do that? Why should she think you'd be interested?" she breathed.

"She's a very wise girl, is Jenny," he smiled. "She guessed I loved you but, until she knew you weren't going to marry Jim, she must have decided it was best to leave things as they were."

"Dear Jenny," Madge whispered.

"I left for Hunsworth early this morning," Miles said. "I went to the Lingard's home first and Mrs. Lingard said you'd come this way with the dog, so I followed. I caught sight of you disappearing over the skyline. A good thing I did, too!"

They said little more as they made their way to the car. When Madge was tucked in the back seat, a rug about her, Miles got in beside her.

"Madge, can't you guess why I came north today?" he asked seriously, turning to look into her face. "It was to beg you to come back to London — to marry me. I can't get on without you. I know that now."

Madge tried to say something, but the words would not come.

Miles grinned at her. Taking a clean handkerchief from his breast pocket, he tenderly rubbed the drying mud from her cheeks.

"Now you're fit to kiss," he murmured, and when she put up no resistance, he drew her into his arms.